PLAY THINGS

PETER PRINCE was born in England and educated both there and in the United States. He is the author of nine novels, including *Adam Runaway* and *Play Things*, which won the Somerset Maugham Award, and several film and television screenplays, including *The Hit*, which starred John Hurt, Tim Roth, and Terence Stamp, and the BAFTA-winning, Emmy-nominated PBS/BBC *Oppenheimer* series. He lives in London with his wife Linda and flies to New York when he can to visit friends and family.

By Peter Prince

Play Things (1972)
Dogcatcher (1974)
Agents of a Foreign Power (1977)
The Good Father (1983)
Death of the Soap Queen (1990)
The Great Circle (1997)
Waterloo Story (1998)
Bubbles (2000)
Adam Runaway (2005)

PETER PRINCE

Play Things

A NOVEL

WITH A NEW FOREWORD BY THE AUTHOR

VALANCOURT BOOKS
Richmond, Virginia
2013

Play Things by Peter Prince
First published London: Gollancz, 1972
First Valancourt Books edition 2013

Copyright © 1972 by Peter Prince
Foreword © 2013 by Peter Prince

The right of Peter Prince to be identified as Author of this work has
been asserted by him in accordance with the Copyright, Designs and
Patents Act 1988.

Published by Valancourt Books, Richmond, Virginia
Publisher & Editor: JAMES D. JENKINS
20th Century Series Editor: SIMON STERN, University of Toronto
http://www.valancourtbooks.com

ISBN 978-1-939140-67-8
Also available as an electronic book

All Valancourt Books publications are printed on acid free paper
that meets all ANSI standards for archival quality paper.

Set in Dante MT 11/13.5

FOREWORD

MANY years ago, in the early 1970s, having quit the academic life just before it quitted me, I took a temporary job as an assistant in an "adventure playground". This was still within the era of innocence and high hopes for the perfectibility of humankind and especially for the natural goodness of children if only they weren't obstructed by the hang-ups and cynicism of the adult world. In fact a strong aroma of flower power hung over the whole venture. Adventure playgrounds were a natural expression of this mood—in surroundings of bucolic charm and ease, "kids and young adults" would disport themselves in relaxed and unconventional physical activities. There would be no organised ball-games or regimented physical jerks; there would be a lot of hanging from ropes and jumping out of trees.

However, as I prepared for my first day in the playground my own hopes and thoughts were not that untroubled. The playground I was going to work at was in what was then a rather tough area of South London (it has since become quite chic.) I feared the worst: challenges to my authority, confrontations, even physical violence. Some of these "kids" I knew were quite big. And I wasn't particularly expert in the arts of either attack or self-defence.

In the event I need not have worried. After a brief settling down period, I got on pretty well with the playground's customers, and with my fellow playleaders. It was a good, happy summer for the most part for both children and adults, and really a tribute to the philosophy of the whole movement. Yet when, a little while after the playground closed for the year, I settled down to write a novel based on my experience, it was rather my first fears that fuelled the narrative drive. So that in the telling my character, the Playleader, became a lonely embattled creature, who finds himself pitted against—and sometimes comically colluding in—the criminal activities of the local children and their adult co-conspirators.

I suppose this was a sort of betrayal of the truth. Yet I think too I was experiencing a widely shared though not yet articulated uneasiness about the whole hippy philosophy. For a few short years the perfectibility of man (and woman) was entertained as a real prospect—as long as you "never trusted anyone over thirty". The history of the world since then has at least shown up the flaws in this lovely but insubstantial dream.

So I think my story of the Playleader and his playground was not good reportage in regard to the brief realities of that time and place—but I think too it expressed the deeper anxieties of the period and what was to come after. In that sense I was as truthful as I could be.

The book came out at last after the usual interminable gap between delivery of the manuscript and publication. It did pretty well: won a prestigious literary prize, introduced me to a number of interesting people in both publishing and film and television making. The latter have mostly financed my subsequent novel writing, as well as sending me to various memorable places: Hollywood, Turkey, Alaska, Spain and Portugal and others. I'm grateful to them all.

As for the children—the "kids" I worked for and played beside in that long ago summer—they will have children themselves by now, maybe grandchildren. I really hope that they are able to trust them in the holidays to anywhere as happy and lively and safe as my old Adventure Playground was.

PETER PRINCE
London
July 31, 2013

6

PLAY THINGS

For Beth

Part One

I

ON MONDAY THE Playground opened. Wednesday the hut burned to the ground. By closing-time Saturday evening three out of the four original playleaders had quit, one at long-distance from a hospital bed.

The survivor sat on an upturned first-aid box and stared thoughtfully at the sinking sun. The Park-keeper stopped his bicycle at the wire fence which divided the Playground from the rest of the park and regarded him kindly.

"Tell you what it is, squire," he said. "You got yourself badly situated here."

"How do you mean?" enquired the Playleader.

"Well," the Park-keeper explained, "you got your blackies over there, haven't you?" He waved towards one side of the park, beyond which rose dark, slum-encrusted slopes. "And you've got all your white people over *there*." Now he pointed to the opposite side of the park where a dozen shimmering pale-grey tower blocks rose thirty storeys high above the trees. "And here *you* are, poor sod. Dead in the middle. No-man's-land."

The Playleader gazed about him. The Playground looked like a conquered province. There, in one corner, were the charred remains of the hut. Directly in front of him, the Playground's fence sported great gaping holes, some apparently torn open by brute force, others professionally created with wire-cutters. A blackened patch on the hill behind him showed where the kids had been imitating the TV news pictures from Belfast by chucking lighted petrol-filled milk bottles at each other and at those set in authority over them. There were even axe-marks on the great oak tree which towered above the centre of the Playground—someone in the night had been trying to hack it down. Several smaller trees had already been successfully reduced to stumps.

The Playleader nodded wearily. "Looks bad, doesn't it?"

A little girl, the last child left in the Playground, was crouching opposite the Playleader, staring up at him. She was about nine.

"You married then?" she asked urgently.

"Yes, I am," the Playleader told her.

"My friend fancies you," said the little girl. "What d'you reckon?"

"I dunno," said the Playleader, "I'd have to see her first."

The Park-keeper now was gazing round the Playground. "By Christ, they really mucked it about, didn't they?" he marvelled.

The Playleader lit a cigarette and wondered whether to phone in his resignation now or in the morning.

"Animals!" said the Park-keeper harshly.

The Playleader looked up at the old man. "How come they don't bust up the park itself?" he asked.

"Oh we have our troubles," said the Park-keeper. "They're always in and out of my flower beds."

"Yeah, but they don't actually take the whole park apart, do they? Not like they've done here."

"Ah no. They wouldn't do that," agreed the Park-keeper. "I'll tell you how we did it, though it's not much use to you now. The fact is, those lads of fourteen or so that are giving you all the trouble—know who I mean?—well, *we* had em first years ago when they was only five or six, see? Now, one step off the grass verge when they're little tykes and it's *bash!*—" He banged his fist onto the fence. "Crack in the mouth!" He hit the fence again. "*And* the next time! *And* the next! And it sort of trains them up you see. So when they're grown up, they're not after messing up my park. In fact, they don't hardly even come into it. But this place here. Brand-new, people they've never seen before in charge—well, it's fair game aint it? Let me tell you," he said, fixing the Playleader with a grandfatherly gaze. "Get em young and bash em hard. It's the only way, the only thing they take any notice of."

The Playleader shuffled his feet awkwardly. He never knew how to deal with this kind of tirade.

"You don't like the idea," the Park-keeper said, nodding sympathetically. "And I know why. They're too bloody big, aren't they?

Some of em'd knock your head off if you tried it on with them. Specially the boogies. By Christ there're some mean sods in that black lot." He shook his head despondently. "I can't really help you my son. Nobody can." He looked once more around the appalling wasteland. "They'll have to close it down."

The Park-keeper cycled slowly off. The Playleader watched him go, then looked down at the little girl who had been tugging at the leg of his jeans for the past few minutes.

"Will you be here tomorrow?" she asked. "I'll bring my friend if you will."

"Yeah, I'll be here," the Playleader said.

2

ON SUNDAYS THE Playground didn't open until noon. However, because of the vast holes in the fence, it could be said that it never really closed, and when the Playleader arrived at twenty past twelve there were already a dozen or so kids inside romping and scuffling in the dirt. Still, he unlocked the gate anyway, and carefully stood the "No Adults allowed in Here" sign upright and facing out towards the park.

None of the kids seemed to notice his arrival. He watched them charge about for a minute or two and then went round to the tiny cabin in the back of the Playground. It was made of thick concrete, and so had stood up reasonably well to the repeated assaults made upon it. Its stout wooden door also still stood firm, though terribly battered. The Playleader unlocked it and stepped inside the hut. Sitting on a pile of thick rope, he very slowly changed into his work boots.

After about ten minutes there was a resounding kick on the door. The Playleader got up and cautiously opened it. A stocky little boy of about six stood on the threshold. "How about gettin out the ropes then?" he shouted angrily.

"I'm just about to," said the Playleader timidly, backing into the room.

"Doesn't matter. I'll do it," the boy said sternly. He grabbed at an end of rope and tugged it after him through the door. The Playleader watched until the last of it was out of the room, then followed it, carefully locking the door behind him.

By the time they and the rope had all got back into the Playground, the little boy was puffing and blowing. He dropped the coil and kicked it. "Heavy old wanker," he observed to the Playleader. He kicked it again, "You'd better get it up the tree now."

The Playleader was doubtful. This particular length of rope was a part of something dubbed the 'tarzan swing'. It was designed to dangle from a branch which projected sixty feet up in the air out of the great tree in the centre of the Playground. He had avoided having anything of importance to do with it during the week before, leaving it to the other playleaders, only sometimes lending a hand at some very minor stage of its erection. It was a job that needed two grown people at least, for at one point whoever clambered up the tree to tie the knot on the branch had to depend practically for his life on another rope held taut by some responsible person on the ground. The Playleader looked at the crowd of children that surrounded him expectantly, and shook his head. "Not the tarzan rope today," he announced. "We'll just put the little ones up."

There was a howl of rage.

"I'm sorry," said the Playleader, "but you see there's no-one to hold the rope for me."

"I'll hold it," said the tiny lad who had brought the rope into the Playground. The Playleader smiled indulgently.

An older boy said, "Go on, chief, we'll *all* hold on for you. You'll be all right." Everyone applauded.

"No, it's too risky," said the Playleader, flustered.

"Aaaah—scared cunt!" scoffed another boy. "I'll go up it. I aint afraid."

"Yeah, let Foxy go up!" the crowd shouted.

"No, you can't." The Playleader shook his head. "I'm not allowed to put you in danger like that. It's in the book."

"Well, what's it to be, chief? Foxy or you?"

"Not Foxy," said the Playleader firmly.

"Up you get then, chief."

First he had to tie a piece of string around a stone, then the other end of the string around one end of the rope. After four or five tries, he got the stone cleanly through the angle between the branch and the tree trunk. The stone took the string along just far enough for him to be able to pull it and the attached rope end through the angle. He lined up a half-dozen of the bigger boys to hold one end of the rope firm. Then he leaped clumsily up the other end, scrabbling with his feet against the tree bark, and propelling himself very slowly upwards. He saw the group of boys below sway against the strain of his weight. They shouted gleefully to see the peril he was in.

Thirty dreadful feet up in the air, the Playleader thought of how much he hated heights and how little he liked children. He had stuck with the job throughout the terrible week before only because he had worked in a factory all through the winter, and now yearned to earn his money in the open-air for a month or two. But for a broken back, he thought miserably as the squeals of delight rose from below, it really wasn't worth it.

Ineptly and painfully, the Playleader at last reached the high branch. His spirits reviving, he looked down cheerfully at the upturned faces far below, while a cool breeze soothed his heated brow. Then he wriggled gingerly along the smooth branch, pushing the rope before him, until he reached a patch of canvas lagging. He turned the rope end several times around the bough and then achieved a number of bulging and inexpert knots. "Give it a tug," he yelled below. Five of them dived onto the rope at once. It creaked and strained, but held. In a small glow of triumph the Playleader slid down the sixty feet of rope. His hands hurt horribly by the time he reached the ground.

Immediately a long queue formed to use the tarzan swing. This happened every day, all through the day. For it was by far the greatest thing in the Playground. It was beautifully simple to use. Two high wooden pedestals stood facing each other on either side of the tall tree, many yards apart. One climbed on one of these, gripped the rope, then took off on a tremendous sweeping arc towards the other pedestal far away. On the first morning the Playground had opened, the Playleader had had a couple of goes on the tarzan rope. It had been a beautiful experience. The closest thing to it, he thought, was skiing; it had the same sweet combination of speed and lightness. He watched for a while now as the first passenger of the day zipped whooping through the air. It looked as good as ever. He resolved to have another go himself when he'd finished putting up the other rope. Providing nothing awkward had turned up before then.

At one o'clock the Playleader was finishing putting up the last rope, on a tree which stood near where the hut used to be. It wasn't very high, but it was a tricky job. To get up on the branch, he had to leap up against the broad tree trunk and heave himself upwards using only the shallowest of hand and footholds. Then he had to hump himself laboriously along the bough towards the canvas where the rope end would be tied, his legs drooping down on either side. There was a nasty swelling on the branch half-way down. Every time, it was even chances that he would land uncomfortably upon it.

As in fact he did today, sending sickening pains through his crutch and into his stomach. He rested his sweating forehead against the bark; the noise of the Playground a dim hub-hub in his ears.

One clear voice cut through it. "I've brought her," it said. "Her name's Gloria."

The Playleader peered blearily down to see on the ground below the small girl who had spoken to him the evening before. She was pointing to another little girl, pale and faintly pretty with golden hair, who was standing simpering about eight paces away. The Playleader settled his head on the bough again.

"Do you fancy her then?" demanded the voice below. "You know she does you."

"Oooh I *don't!*" shouted Gloria, embarrassed.

"Yes yer do," her friend said with scorn. "Well. What's the matter with her?" she called up to the Playleader.

"Nothing," he said, looking across at Gloria, "she seems very nice."

"There you are Gloria," said the other little girl, in a rather bitter voice, *"you're* all right."

Gloria then burst into tears and ran away. The Playleader, who had got over the pain in his balls and was beginning to enjoy the little comedy, was taken aback. "What's up with her?" he asked.

Gloria's friend looked up at him stonily. "Stupid little cow!" she snapped at length. "I told her you was married, and she can't get over it." The child walked a little way away, then turned back to watch the Playleader who was once more edging his way down the branch. "It wouldn't bother me though," she said quietly. Then she ran back to the tree, her face contorted in rage, shouting so piercingly that he had to clap his hands to his ears, and clasp his thighs to the bough to keep from falling off. "But I'm no fuckin Gloria am I?" she shrieked. And then, as the Playleader cowered terrified up in his tree, she scampered off after her playmate.

The big kids, the governors, arrived half-way through the afternoon, after the Playleader had had a sandwich and a drink of tea from his flask and when he was thinking seriously of having a go on the tarzan rope. They came over from the council block side of the park. There were eight of them, their ages ranging from about thirteen to sixteen. All wore more or less the same outfits: little snap-brimmed hats, long dark overcoats, even though it was a warmish day, and nattily flared trousers. Some still wore the old heavy boots, the rest had on steel-tipped shoes.

They came sweeping across the Playground in a line abreast, about five yards apart from one another. The Playleader had to admit to himself that it looked dramatic—the eight samurai. The Playground was quiet. The other children had scuttled into far corners for safety. For the first time that day, the tarzan rope hung still. The Playleader was incredibly scared.

They converged on where he was standing, strategically near the gate. One of them came up very close. The Playleader backed away. "Come on," the boy said disgustedly. "I aint gonna hit cha . . . Where're the others of you then?"

"I'm the only one," quavered the Playleader. I'll have to run, he thought. I'm not going to get my face messed up. "The others didn't come today," he said. He stepped back another pace.

"You off too, are yer, squire?" said another boy evilly.

"You might as well," the first boy said. He looked around him. "Not much left here. Few ropes and bits and pieces. Rubbish! Yeah, I'd fuck off if I was you, mate." He watched the Playleader, daring him to take him at his word. The Playleader had no idea what to do. He wondered if he could get workingman's compensation.

"'It 'im, Denis," one of the older boys called softly, "Duff 'im propah!" The Playleader, fascinated, watched the boy in front of him begin to waver on his feet like a cat about to strike. The Playleader's hand convulsively clutched something square and solid in his pocket. He brought it out and thrust it at the trembling boy in front of him.

"Have a cigarette," he whispered. "Have a lot." Denis blinked, stared at the Playleader's outstretched hand, then sank back on his heels, and took the cigarette packet. There were about sixteen, seventeen inside. The other kids crowded around Denis, who gave them one each and then dropped the packet in his overcoat pocket. They stood in front of the Playleader in a line, a cigarette poking from each mouth.

"Got a light?" asked Denis.

The Playleader lit each of them up. His hand, he noticed, was quite OK, steady as a rock. Denis took a couple of drags and smiled cordially at the Playleader. "I told you I wasn't goin to hit cha." The Playleader smiled back. "We come for the ropes," Denis went on. "We need em."

The boys watched the Playleader narrowly. "Ah, not the ropes," the Playleader begged.

"'Fraid so," said Denis, shaking his head.

"All of them?"

"Yep. We need the lot. For towing," he added mysteriously.

"*Not* the tarzan rope."

"Oh yes. We need that big fucker most of all." Denis pitched his fag into the dirt and ground it to shreds with an elegant black suede shoe. "Don't take it hard, mate," he said. Then, turning to the others, "Right. Let's have em down!"

The Playleader watched as they fetched down the ropes he had put up so laboriously a few hours before. Some of the younger children came over to stand near him. "Aren't you going to stop them?" they asked. He didn't answer. Denis, up high in the tall tree, untying the tarzan rope, caught sight of the Playleader watching him, and waved cheerily. Soon all the ropes were down. Denis commandeered some of the smaller kids to carry them in his train. He stopped by the Playleader on his way out and gave him a cigarette.

"Aren't you going to bring the ropes back?" the Playleader asked.

"No," said Denis firmly. "Definitely not." The procession moved exuberantly off. The children who had stood with the Playleader earlier now ran after it, begging to be allowed to help carry the ropes. With a mild pang, the Playleader noticed Gloria and her pal among the deserters. When everyone else had gone, he wandered around the Playground picking up a few discarded toys and games. At four o'clock, two hours before the proper closing time, he locked the gates and went home.

3

FOR ONCE HIS wife was there before him. "Hello," she called. "I'm up to my ears in proofs."

The Playleader peered inside the refrigerator, looking for a snack.

"I'm in here," Alice called. "The bedroom."

There was nothing in the fridge. He went in to see her. She was sitting up in bed, propped against some cushions, wearing her horn-rimmed glasses, clutching a ball-point pen and, as she'd said, surrounded by galley-proofs.

"It's this poetry man's book," she said brightly. "I *have* to finish it tonight. But he's such a bore I keep dozing off." She was looking very pretty, the Playleader thought. She asked him about his day. He told her.

"Oh Christ," she said, "they'll close it down now, won't they?"

"I s'pose so," he said.

She frowned, looked down at the proof on her lap, changed an h to an H and said "So what now? What will you do?"

He rolled on his back on the bed.

"You've no idea have you?" she said, a glint of anger in her voice. She stared at him critically. He didn't answer. She pouted and went back to her proof, impatiently scoring out a repeated line. He picked up another galley from the mess strewn on the eiderdown and read a few lines.

"All right!" she said, watching his expression, "it's mostly rubbish. But at least he *produces*. You should think of that."

"Bully for him."

"It's *so* important," she said, leaning over to wipe a smudge from his cheek. "It's so sad to watch you stumbling from one thing to another. It spoils things for me too you know."

"I had a job," he said sullenly, "but they took my fucking ropes away. I can't help that."

She shook her head. "Oh come on," she said, "that was a *non*-job. That wasn't for you. And how long would it have lasted? A summer. Then they'd be back at school. And what would you have done?"

"I made money last winter."

"I don't just want you to make money," she said, caressing his hair, "I want you to be *proud* of what you do. And you can't be proud of working in a factory, can you? And you can't be proud of letting little boys steal your ropes, can you?"

"They were big mothers, some of those little boys," he muttered, squashing his face against her knee.

"There's such a lot you could do," she carried on, smiling tenderly. "You know I stood by you when you gave everything up. But it's time now. . . . Well, I know so many people who could help you. We'll get you some nice clothes and then some nice interviews. Right now I could get you a job at the office. I know I could swing it."

"No," he said angrily, rolling away from her. She pursued him.

"Not at my place then. But in another company? Come on love, you'd make such a pretty publisher."

He went into another room and sat by the window. He could hear her rustling her proofs crossly in the bedroom. He brooded on the grey street below. He felt in his pocket for his cigarettes. Nothing there.

After a half-hour or so, she came into the room. She had changed into a new skirt and had made up her eyes and done her hair. "I'm off," she said briskly. "It's Women's Lib night tonight. I'm taking the car. OK?" He nodded. She stopped as she was turning to go. "Are you going to be all right?" He nodded again. She came and stood in front of him, her belly on a level with his face as he sat there. He held her to him, sliding his hands up her firm legs, kneading the tight buttocks under his palms. She ruffled his hair. "You're silly," she said. "You *want* to be sad." He clutched her more tightly to him. She tugged his hair. "Come on now," she said, "I'll be late." She pulled his head back, smiling at first, then relaxing into disappointment. "You're into that silly crying trick again," she scolded. "Now you know I'm not going to take any notice of it any more." She wriggled away from him. "Be nice when I come home," she said from the door.

After she had gone he dried his tears, made himself some tea and toast and peanut butter, and watched television until about eleven o'clock, at which time Alice had not yet got home so he went to bed alone.

4

THE NEXT DAY, Monday, the Playleader was back in his Playground. He hadn't expected to be. After slopping around the flat for half the morning, he had remembered to phone in to the Recreation Department to report the latest development at the Playground and to tender his resignation. The man at the other end had said in a motherly tone, "Yes, well, it's always difficult at first, isn't it?"

"No. This is the end," the Playleader had declared.

"Have another go," the man urged.

"No. Christ! It's dangerous down there."

But in the end the Playleader had agreed just to pop over there one more time to straighten things up and to talk it over with someone from the Department. "It could even be me," the man said temptingly.

Down at the Playground not much was stirring. Two boys in

jeans and dirty gym-shoes came over to ask him when the ropes
were going up. The Playleader told them never as far as he was
concerned. They nodded equably and went out of the Playground
through a big new gap in the fence. It was drizzling slightly. The
Playleader turned up his collar and retired to the protection of the
tall tree where the tarzan rope used to hang. A boy of about twelve
stopped on his progress across the Playground and came over to
the sheltering Playleader.

"Here you are, chief," the boy chortled. "Here's one for you.
Right? Are you listening?"

"What to?" asked the Playleader.

"It's a question. You have to answer a question see? OK? Here's
the question. Right? Here it is. Do you like sex and travel? That's
the question. Right? Do you like sex and travel? Now you have to
answer it."

"Yes, I do," said the Playleader.

"Well, fuck off then!" The boy fell about laughing. It was a
good-natured laugh though. The Playleader felt quite fond of the
lad. He offered him a cigarette. The kid took it and then lit them
both up with a heavy steel lighter.

"That's my Zippo," he said, showing the Playleader the lighter.
"I got it from my sister. She lives in America. She's never coming
back."

They smoked companionably as the drizzle grew heavier. After
about three-quarters of an hour, the boy said in a kindly tone,
"Shame about the ropes."

The man from the Recreation Department came at four.

"Couldn't get away any earlier," he called across the Playground.
"Big flap on at the office."

The Playleader had been crouching in a sort of slit trench half-
way up the hill, digging vaguely in the wet mud with a pointed
stick to pass the time. He stood up and walked over to join the man
by the gate.

"Name's Tenby. How are you?" the man said. "I spoke to you on
the phone." He was about thirty-five, greying at the sideburns, but
still hanging in there with his zipped jacket, Donald Duck T-shirt,

and sweepingly flared trousers. "Now," he said, "what exactly is the matter down here?" His eyes travelled over the broken and gutted landscape, past the splintered trees and deep trenches, and rested finally on the charred remains of the hut. "Christ!" he said at last. "Passchendaele!"

Looking around with him, the Playleader had to admit that the Playground, seen through the drizzling grey rain, had seldom looked worse.

"They've really done this place over properly," marvelled Tenby. He shook his head. "Little cunts! I'm so glad I haven't got any of my own. Have you? . . . Right for you! I hate the little buggers, *hate* em!" He kicked at a blackened log nearby. "I wouldn't have your job at any price."

The Playleader pulled the Playground keys out of his pocket and tried to hand them over. Tenby wouldn't take them.

"Please! I don't want to be a Playleader any more."

Tenby placed an avuncular arm around his shoulder. "I'll tell you how it is," he said cosily, "I'd *like* to say to you—'right, close it up, shut it down, go back home, and thanks for everything'—but . . . I *can't*." He began to walk across the Playground, guiding the Playleader with his arm. "Now you know my boss Harrison, don't you? He probably hired you. Didn't he? Yes, well, therein lies our problem. Between you and me, though it's an open secret, we're not dealing with a rational man with Harrison here. You probably know something of his career. No? No reason why you should. Suffice to say, he's faced a lot of opposition over the years, he's taken a lot of stick. You can read about it in his book. I'll get you a copy. Suffice to say once again, it's all made him a bit *weird*." They paused by a particularly gaping rip in the wire fence. "Bastards!" snarled Tenby. They resumed their walk.

"I wish you'd take the keys," grumbled the Playleader.

"No, I won't take the keys," Tenby said firmly. "Not until I've put you thoroughly in the picture. *Then* we'll see if you still want to give them to me. Who knows? Perhaps you won't after all." The rain was heavy again. The Playleader led his companion over to the tall tarzan rope tree. Sodden, weary, the Playleader sneezed several times. "I want to go home soon," he said miserably.

"Harrison," Tenby said thoughtfully. "An extraordinary man. I wish you knew him. You'd understand me so much better. He's done amazing things. I mean—one hates him of course, but one can't but admire him. In ten years, from less than scratch, he's built up—do you *know* how many of these darn playgrounds there are in this borough? Seventeen! You're the seventeenth in fact. Do you *know* how many staff there are working on this programme? You wouldn't believe it, if I told you. And the budget! Scores of thousands and it goes up every year. They don't dare touch it. The amount of publicity this programme gets is *phenomenal*. We're sacrosanct; unstoppable!" He put his arm once more around the Playleader's shoulders. The Playleader, inattentively lighting a damp cigarette, started guiltily.

"I can't tell you," Tenby was saying, "how much this playground thing has meant in my own career. I started with very few advantages, you know. I did rather badly at university. They didn't make me an officer on National Service. I was dogged by a rotten accent. I could have sunk without a trace. Especially in the civil service. But, as you can see, I haven't sunk at all. Thanks to Harrison, I'm a coming man. My grade, my salary—both beautiful—and nicest of all I've become an expert on this playground lark. I've been on television about it. I'm invited to write in the specialist journals on it. And in the not so specialist too. Do you take *New Society?* Well . . . if you did you might have noticed my name. A couple of little pieces recently. I did them off the top of my head but they went down very well. I can send you some copies if you like? . . . Anyway . . . the *point* of it all is that all this, all this money, and all these jobs and my career too, rests on this playground programme. *It can't be allowed to fail.* You understand that surely?"

The Playleader nodded glumly.

"Now," Tenby resumed, "like I say, if it were me I'd say, 'OK. We've made a bloomer here. Close it up. Pay off the playleader— with perhaps an extra little something for being so brave and patient—and we'll be content for the time being with just *sixteen* playgrounds. What's one playground more or less?' *I'd* say. But—" his hand tightened on the Playleader's shoulder "—we're dealing with *Harrison*, not with me. And *he* doesn't close down *any* playgrounds. *He* believes—rightly or wrongly I couldn't say—that you *cannot* contract, that it's all *up* if you contract. *He* says our enemies—and we have plenty, you know, snapping at our heels all the time, worrying at our budget—he says they're just waiting for any sign, *any* sign that the programme's slowing up, dying away, becoming effete. *He* says—God, he does!—that there's only one way for any healthy organism. And that's *up*, *up*, *up*! *He* wants *expansion, conquest*; he doesn't want to hear of a playground closing *down*, he wants to hear of twenty more opening *up*. His very words." Tenby smiled indulgently. "He's quite the little Hitler, isn't he? And in a good cause, why not?"

He looked across at the Playleader, slumped sadly against the tree trunk. Tenby sighed. "Won't you give it another try?" he begged.

The Playleader shook his head. Then shook it again. "No," he said.

Tenby stared up at the sullen sky. "We're not going to close it," he said. "It's an impossibility."

"That's OK," said the Playleader. "Go ahead. Keep it open. But get somebody else to run it."

"We *can't*," Tenby snapped. "I've phoned around for playleaders all over the city. They're frightened. They heard about what happened here last week. They won't do it."

"Well," said the Playleader, "it *did* happen. I saw it all . . . and it could have been *me* if I hadn't kept out of the way."

"Shit," said Tenby. He strode out ten paces into the rain. Then returned in haste to the tree. He held out his hands, imploring. "Don't you see my problem? I can't go back to the office leaving it like this. I can't recommend closure. Don't you see that? Won't you help? Stay awhile?"

"I *can't*," the Playleader said emotionally. "Don't *you* see? It's dangerous here. I'm all alone. I'm exposed . . . And I've got no gift with kids anyway. Look, I'd probably have quit whatever happened. I'm just not the type. You don't want me. It's a mistake."

"Oh *stay*!" Tenby cried. "Look . . . maybe—maybe some extra money?" His face was contorted in a kind of agony. "I shouldn't—I don't like to . . . but I suppose it might just be possible . . . after all, there's only one of you now, there should be four, we'll save on the budget anyway . . . All right. How about it? Some more money? You'd stay?"

The Playleader started to shake his head, to turn down the offer. Then he stopped. An idea was growing in his mind. "How much money?" he asked cautiously.

Tenby was at once assured again, buoyant, impudent. "Every man to his price, eh?" He made a business of thinking over the Playleader's question. "How much?" he mused. "How much? Well . . . fiver do? Fiver a week?"

The Playleader thought it over. Was it enough? Perhaps not? What he wanted might well cost more. "Ten?" he asked.

Tenby wrinkled his nose. "Ooooh. . . ." He shook his head doubtfully, hunched his shoulders, folded his arms, bent his knees . . . then as suddenly unwound himself and said softly, "OK."

"And I'll definitely need some help at weekends," said the Playleader doggedly.

"*Somewhere* I'll find it for you." Tenby was extravagantly relieved. "God!" he breathed. "Christ knows what I'd have done if . . . Harrison! That man can be so *vicious*! Wow!" He clutched the Playleader by the shoulders again. "You're doing a beautiful thing," he enthused. "I won't *ever* forget it."

"I need the first ten quid now."

Tenby peeled off a five and five ones from the thick wad he took from his trouser pocket. "Now don't let me down," he warned. The Playleader stuck the banknotes in the top pocket of his denim jacket. They walked together to the gates.

"When do I get the new equipment?" the Playleader asked. "New hut, paint, table-tennis, ropes . . . when do I get all them?"

"No problem," Tenby beamed. "You should see this immense bulging warehouse we've got beside the river. Impossible to find a use for most of the stuff. It's rotting away. Thousands of quids' worth. That's partly why we have to keep setting up new playgrounds . . . We'll get you the ropes etcetera tomorrow. The hut, I should think, a day later." He looked disgustedly down at the remains of the previous structure. "We'll have a concrete one this time, eh? Burning's too easy; we'll make the little farts use their initiatives."

At the gate, Tenby stopped suddenly, his brow furrowed in thought. "Listen," he said, "are there any chances of getting a demonstration off the ground here?"

The Playleader stared in amazement. Tenby said excitedly, "It's a nice idea. About thirty or so local mums, babies in prams, you know, and kids holding signs 'Save our playground', you know, and 'Let our kiddies play'. Something for the papers. This would be very nice for Harrison. And nice for me too. What do you think? Got any local contacts?"

"No."

"Councillors? Local journalists? School teachers?"

"I don't know anyone. Nobody knows me. Nobody knows the Playground, as far as I can see. Except the kids, of course."

"OK," Tenby said, resignedly. "Shame. It could have been nice."

The Playleader watched Tenby's jaunty figure disappearing down the park lane that ran outside the Playground. Then he turned and walked around the Playground, still unexpectedly his. The rain had stopped now. Its long stay had managed to gentle slightly the rough, torn earth, had made the scarred bark of the trees gleam and the grass and leaves damply fresh. Amazingly, it didn't look half bad. Looking about him, touching for reassurance the folded banknotes in his pocket, the Playleader felt for the first time a strange, sneaking pride of ownership.

5

THE GOOD FEELING stayed with the Playleader when he went home at five, and on the whole it survived until Alice got in at nearly ten. She blamed the tube for her lateness. She'd been stuck at Earl's Court "for ages". She'd been there, she said, with a sidelong look at the Playleader, perhaps for fifty minutes. Of course, she conceded, she hadn't been able to get away from the office very early—"that fucking poetry man" had held her up. He was on television tonight. He was meant to plug the book. She really ought to watch it.

She eyed him curiously at the end of her apologies. "You look cheerful," she said.

"I had a good day, a nice day," he told her happily. "A *productive* day."

"Hm . . ." she watched him. "Did you quit? Is the playground thing over?"

"No," he said brightly, "I've worked it all out. It's staying open and I'm staying on. I've got this plan, you see . . ."

"Shit," she said, disgusted. "I thought you really were going to make a clean break for once." She bustled angrily about the apartment, picking up old newspapers and dirty clothes from the floor, and sweeping up some screws lying on the carpet where he had been mending the stereo. "I'm not going to nag you," she called from the kitchen. "You're not going to make me. But you *know* you're just into the same old pattern again. Drift, drift. Where does it get you? Nowhere. Right? . . . Right?"

When he didn't answer her, she came into the sitting-room and gazed at him slumped in the arm-chair. She said softly, "You think I'm getting at you. But you're getting at me too. . . . You know that?"

"It's unintentional," he said at last.

"I don't know," she said. They were silent then. After a while she went back to the kitchen. "Have you eaten yet?" she called. She wanted the quarrel over.

"No," he mumbled. Then loudly, so she could hear him, "No. What are we having?"

She hesitated. "Oh . . . I've eaten. What would *you* like? I've got . . . eggs," she ended on a surprised note. "That's all we've got."

"I'll have eggs," he said. "Scrambled please."

She suggested he had it with her in front of the television. A nice idea. He got out the little side-table, planted it opposite the TV set, dressed it with a mat, plates, cup and saucer. Alice brought in the eggs. He put on the television and tuned it to BBC-2. They watched the fuzzy flickering end of the previous programme.

"So what is this thing you want to watch?"

"Some panel game. I watched the taping. It's the first of a series and he's got a regular spot. It's . . . quite good. It's a cultural sort of a panel game. You might like it."

She was sipping a cup of coffee, staring anxiously at the TV screen. He looked across at her sympathetically. Clearly her day had been a long one. She was tired and her clothes were creased and wrinkled. Even so, she was lovely to look at. Watching her, he felt a familiar pride that he had her. Well, that he was married to her. He said, "It sounds fine. It sounds interesting."

She smiled across at him gratefully, "Probably not," she said.

It was awful. He couldn't understand the game, and the panel was vile—terrible people, a trad English mixture of incompetence, self-importance, and sarcasm. It was all vaguely to do with testing their knowledge of Eng. Lit. But nobody knew anything at all, and the Chairman of the game, a fashionable literary buffoon, was quite thrown off balance by their ignorance and steered the show with fatal incompetence. Alice's poetry man was among the worst, grotesquely vain and stupid beyond rescue. Alice, however, watched him intently, continuing to do so even after he had managed to slip in a reference to his forthcoming book.

"Wow, awful crap, eh?" the Playleader said conversationally about two-thirds through the programme.

"Sssh!" hissed Alice balefully, leaning forward in her chair to watch her man fail to guess the author of *Middlemarch*. The Playleader sulked for a while and, when that went unnoticed, glumly watched the show through to the end. It closed finally in a burst of boorish ragging among the contestants, none of whom seemed cast down by their performances. Alice stared contemplatively as their balding, sneering faces faded from the screen. Then she roused herself and smiled across at her husband. "Well," she said, "what do you think? How did he come over?"

"Lousy," said the Playleader casually. "He stank. Like his poems."

To his surprise, she was angry. "Oh, fuck you," she snapped, getting up, snatching her coffee cup. "Tearing down, tearing down! Aren't you *great* at that?"

She stamped off to the kitchen leaving him with dreadful, fast-maturing suspicions. He was no fool. He knew what these late nights and angry outbursts were all about. How could anyone defend such a creep, he thought, unless . . . ? He felt terrible. The idea of his lovely Alice wasting herself on that twat was horrible beyond measure. Personality apart, he was disgustingly old for her. "Winter lying down with spring" he mused, morosely and poetically. . . . He couldn't bear it. "Alice!" he called out in anguish.

He hurried into the kitchen where his wife was gazing into the mirror that was fastened to the wall beside the sink. She turned round quickly, consternation and guilt clear upon her face. He stood before her, raising his hands as if to help her. "I want you to tell me," he implored.

She put a hand to her soft curling hair. "What?" she asked painfully. "Maybe I can't."

"Are you screwing with that . . . poet?"

She looked up at his face, first blankly, then with glee. "Oh no!" she laughed wildly. She took his arms and wrapped them round her and buried her face in his neck. "You stupid! Of course I'm not. What a thing! How could you think it?"

He couldn't believe he was wrong. "I felt it," he said. "And you're so late in all the time. And so restless when you are in."

She was silent, holding him tight.

"But I was wrong?"

"You're crazy," she said fondly. "Do you really think he's my type then? Do you?" She bridled playfully. "Don't you think I could do a lot better?"

"That's what I thought," he said, stroking her smooth forehead and her hair.

For the rest of the evening, before they went to bed, Alice was gay and humorous, every now and then bursting into laughter and coming over to pat him fondly or to tell him some anecdote to illustrate how much more vile her poet was than the Playleader could even have imagined. He believed her denial utterly. He still didn't feel entirely safe, however.

6

DENIS WAS INSIDE the Playground when the Playleader arrived next morning. His full complement of guards was not with him—just one other youth, sitting beside him on a log, thumbing a comic book—but the Playleader was nervous, and wished he'd had time first to plot his approach. But at least now, he thought, things would be settled one way or the other very quickly. Denis looked up as the Playleader approached. He seemed surprised.

"Morning," said the Playleader, shaking out three cigarettes and lighting up, in proper order, first Denis, then his mate, then himself.

"Fancy you being here still," Denis said.

"Yeah, well . . ." mumbled the Playleader, "got to keep the old Playground open, right?"

Denis looked around him. "What's the point? Not much left, is there?"

"Well . . . pretty soon, it's really going to get good," the Playleader enthused. "You see, we're going to get a new hut, concrete this time, and lots of things like table tennis and modelling clay, and so on." He glanced sidelong at Denis's impassive face. "And we're going to get some new ropes up on the trees."

Denis sighed. "I'll have to take em down again, squire." He brooded over his dwindling cigarette. "I can't seem to make it clear to you," he said wearily at last. "We don't like havin you here. You're in the fuckin way. And you'll get fuckin hurt if you stay around."

Denis's mate tittered over his comic book, turned another page. The Playleader sat still, gathering up his forces.

"Look man," he said, "I'm willing to pay over some protection if you like. A fair bit too."

Denis looked at him uncomprehending.

"There'll be a few quid in it." The Playleader thought quickly. "I can go up to five," he said. "No more." It would leave a clear fiver a week on what Tenby was paying him. He looked hopefully at Denis.

"I don't get you," the boy said. "What's this 'protection'?"

"Come on, man . . ." The Playleader was a little impatient. He felt he had the initiative now. "You watch the gangster films on TV, don't you? Protection. *You* know. Eliot Ness. *Hawaii 5-o.* Come on." Denis was looking quite startled. The Playleader spelled it out for him. "I'll pay you five pounds every week. OK? In return you protect the Playground for me."

"Against what?"

"Against *yourself*, of course. It's a good deal, man. You can make some money out of all this power you've got instead of just fucking around destroying things for the hell of it. What do you say?"

Denis was impressed. "Fuck!" he marvelled. "You'd really pay us five a week?"

"If you'd let the Playground alone I would."

"What do you thinka that, Collins?" Denis turned to the boy next to him.

"What, we all get even splits Den, then?" Collins asked hopefully.

"Well, you'd get a bit perhaps," Denis said thoughtfully, staring at the Playleader.

"Yeah, that's right," said the Playleader, trying to catch Collins' eye. "You can all share in it. You can buy enough fags for everybody for the week. Or whatever you want. Go to the pictures. Just as you like."

"Yeah, well, I'll decide all that," Denis said coldly. "Right, Collins?"

"Right, Den," the other said humbly. Denis turned back to the Playleader. "So when do we get paid first?"

"You can start now if you want." The Playleader hesitated. "You'd be stupid to take the money and then let me down. You'd be fucking up a steady income."

"I know all that. Give us the money."

The Playleader counted out five pound notes into Denis's palm. "Nice!" breathed Collins peering over his leader's shoulder. When the money had all changed hands, the Playleader looked up at Denis, who was gazing ahead of him half-smiling.

"Feel good?" asked the Playleader with interest.

Denis's face broke into an ecstatic grin. "Fantastic!" he cried.

The ropes and the other play equipment arrived that afternoon as Tenby had promised. The pre-fabricated segments of the hut weren't due until Wednesday. But before then the Playground had been resurrected. Under Denis's indulgent eye, the Playleader festooned the trees with the new set of ropes. The table-tennis was set up on a piece of land where the old hut had stood. Now cleared of ashes and rubble, it proved ideally flat. Soon games of 2 and 3 a side were going full blast. To add to the fun, the Playleader got out of the little concrete cabin half a dozen tins of paint of different hues, and a dozen paint brushes of various sizes. Throughout the sunny day there was a queue of children waiting to use the brushes, and soon the fallen logs dotted all around the Playground and the lower portions of the living trees too were covered with coat after coat. It all looked very gay.

Now, the Playleader had no particular practical skills; he was really quite unsuited for the job, as his late colleagues in the Playground had often remarked. He couldn't do carpentry, not even of the simplest kind. The rope knots he tried to tie very often, and often dangerously, slipped and fell apart. He couldn't even dig very efficiently in the soft Playground earth.

All this incapacity invited, and had got, much hard contemptuous comment from the kids during the first hours of the Playground's rejuvenation. And on the following day their impatience rose to such heights that they urgently took the tools and ropes out of the Playleader's clumsy hands and did the jobs themselves. The Playleader panicked at first as he read through the relevant paragraphs in the Recreation Department's *Employees' Manual of Conduct*. But he soon decided that it could all come under the phrase "proper supervision at all times", and taking up a position under a shady tree, he settled down to watch the amazingly efficient hive of children as they scurried about hanging beautifully-knotted ropes (except from the tarzan tree, which he reluctantly reserved for himself), and pushing up fantastically impressive, psychedelically-painted shanties.

Even Denis was impressed by the latter, commandeering from its builders one lemon-yellow and pink shack for his own uses. "No squire," he said firmly to the Playleader who tried to protest weakly that their contract had been broken by this action. "I got to have my office here, don't I?" And from then on Denis spent much time in the hot little hut, often counting through the five pound-notes, and checking the entry in the little ledger book he had swiped from W. H. Smith's: "For protection, playground—£5."

7

ON THE AFTERNOON of the day before the new hut arrived, the Park-keeper paid a visit to the Playground. He hung over the fence and gloomily surveyed the thriving scene. The Playleader, who had re-established relations with Gloria's friend, was over watching her play table-tennis, and sucking on a sherbet dip she had brought him after lunch. When he saw the Park-keeper he waved and came over.

"We get the hut tomorrow," he called as he approached the fence.

The Park-keeper wrinkled his nose. "They're making a helluva mess in there," he complained. "It's not good enough, you know."

The Playleader looked round at the teeming Playground, at the children painting and building and playing. "Oh they're all right," he said gently, "they're just having a good time."

"All very well to say that," grumped the old man. "All very well if you're *temporary* here, I dare say. But I know who's going to be in there this winter havin to straighten it all out. Gawd knows what it'll look like at the end of the summer . . . Look at that little bugger wiv the spade!"

"He's just making a drainage system for the bottom of the hill," protested the Playleader after looking behind him again.

"He's makin a blasted lot of extra work for some poor sod!" half-shouted the Park-keeper. The Playleader, head bowed, was silent. The old man seemed soothed by his outburst.

"Not your fault, I suppose," he said, almost kindly. "You're doin your best. You're just not familiar with the 'uman material you've got in there." His eyes drifted over past the Playleader's left shoulder. "'Uman filth too and all." The Playleader turned to see two small West Indian boys chasing a football. He sighed.

"Which reminds me," said the Park-keeper, a note of excitement in his voice, "what I really stopped here for was to give you a warning. I seen some big sambos in the trees back there coming this way. Four or five of em. Big uns."

"Oh, I'm sure it'll be all right," lied the Playleader, not sure at all.

"Yeah," said the Park-keeper derisively, "you better take cover mate." He squinted over into the Playground. "You got some big white lads in there too. I see that young Denis Riley." He shook his head. "Slaughter. There'll be fuckin slaughter." He swung his leg energetically over his bicycle. "I'm leavin you to it. If you're fool enough to stay."

The Playleader nervously hung around the table tennis. There was not long to wait. After about five minutes a group of blacks came through the Playground entrance. The Playleader recognised their leader from the whirling tumult of the first disastrous week. His name was Harmon, he was about fifteen years old, and he had, the Playleader had heard, nine brothers and sisters.

Now he was crooking his finger in the Playleader's direction. "Come over here, man," he called. The Playleader went. Harmon introduced him all around with a sweep of his long arm. "Ray, Facey, Thompson, Danny, and me, Harmon . . . Give 'im a pull on the wine, Facey man." Facey silently handed over a nearly-full bottle of V.P. wine. The Playleader had a little sip. Harmon beamed down on him.

"Listen," he said, "I heah you're handin out cash for this protection shit."

"Well . . ." said the Playleader hesitantly.

"That fuckin Riley go' a fiver off 'im," said the boy called Thompson. His accent was deep south London, in contrast to his leader's lilting West Indian.

"*Raas*, Thompson man," Harmon said sternly. He turned back to the Playleader, smiling broadly once more. "I think we oughta cut in on it, man," he said. "We'll take five too. And we'll give you some *good* protection. OK?"

The Playleader sighed. Luckily he had stuffed his wallet full in the morning. "How many more people will I have to pay off?" he asked, getting it out.

"Oh, there's no more, man," Harmon told him earnestly.

"This'll take care of *everybody*." He held out his hand. The Play-leader put a five pound note into it. That wiped out all his profit from Tenby. The bottle circulated and they all drank a toast to the transaction. Then the boys, with civil farewells to the Playleader, passed on into the rest of the Playground. As Harmon was passing the lemon-yellow and pink shack, Denis came out. The Playleader held his breath.

"Hi," said Denis.

"Ho," said Harmon. And they slapped hands and crawled matily back inside the hut together, Harmon clutching tight at the neck of the bottle of V.P. wine.

8

THE PLAYLEADER SOON reconciled himself to paying out two batches of protection money, and went home that night in a cheer-ful frame of mind. The Playground was shaping up into a success, and he took some pride in this; he felt that, in an imperceptible sort of way, he was helping it go in that direction. It was true that most of the kids hardly seemed to notice his existence. None had said goodbye at the end of the day, except for Gloria's friend (intensely) and Harmon and Denis, on their way out together (calm nods). Still, no-one seemed actually to *mind* him, and that—after all that had gone before—was a big thing. And the protection deal, even with Harmon cutting in on it, had been a real coup. He really believed it.

However, in bed that night (she had crept in at about eleven) it was clear that Alice didn't think so at all when, during his good-night fag, he described the events of the two previous days.

Snuggled up against her warm flesh, he could feel the impa-tience coursing through her.

"Oh, you are *absurd*," she hissed. For some reason they whis-pered after lights out.

"No, Alice," he tugged at her. "It's a very good thing. For the first time there's guaranteed peace down there. And *I* arranged it. I feel *good* about it."

"It's the weakest thing I ever heard," she snapped. "And so unkind to those poor kids. What are you *doing* down in that Playground? Your brain's softening. You're teaching them to be *criminals*."

"Oh, Alice—"

"I mean." She slapped the pillows in her irritation. "It's so fantastic that *you* should actually be teaching *them* how to blackmail *you*. It's incredible!"

"It's not blackmail," he whispered sullenly.

"It's crooked whatever . . . I mean, you know I hate to put it in words but really . . . when I think of myself working damn hard all day long and paying all those sodding taxes so that people like you can squander it on training kids to grow up criminals . . . I really don't think it's funny."

"Alice!" he raised himself to look at her in the gloom. She was staring at the ceiling. "You're really getting weird, Alice," he said.

She turned to him. "Well," she said flatly, "perhaps. But your attitude . . . there's a lack of maturity in you. It gets me down."

He hardly listened, pleased that her inexplicable anger had passed. She lay now turned away from him. He threaded his hands past her arms to settle on her flat stomach and graze at the soft fleece just below. He thought to please her: "Let's fuck."

She did not turn to him. "No," she said, "I don't want to."

"Course you do," he teased her. "You always do."

"No. Not this time."

His fingers searched inside her. It was true. She was dry and unwelcoming. Crestfallen, he settled back on his side of the bed. They lay back to back, a wide space between.

9

THE TRUCK ARRIVED at the Playground at lunchtime on the following day. A half-dozen men climbed down, hawking and spitting into the dust. There was a flurry of activity, shouts, orders, curses. Soon the truck was moving off again, leaving behind a number of slabs of concrete and a man who introduced himself to the Playleader as "Straker". When the truck had disappeared, Straker, after a quick, interested glance round the Playground, whipped out a steel comb, flicked back the sides of his hair, winked at the Playleader, and produced a yard-long folding pack of porno pictures.

"Now these aren't my best," he said, "but they'll give you an idea. Course they're only samples."

"How much?" asked the Playleader, checking through the collection.

Straker eyed him thoughtfully. "50p a snap. Delivery within the month."

"I'll take this one . . . and this one," the Playleader pointed.

"You like the dikes, I see," Straker grinned, accepting a pound note from the Playleader. "And fond of animals too. Not my taste. Not my taste at all."

"Now you'll have to put em away," the Playleader said, gesturing at the children who were milling around the concrete slabs. "You can't let them see em."

"Oh just one or two of the big ones," Straker protested, pointing out the tall figures of Thompson and Denis Riley on the edges of the crowd.

"No, man, really," the Playleader insisted. "I just can't let you. You know I got these rules I have to follow. You can show em outside the gate, can't you?"

"Well," said Straker grumpily, but putting away his photographs, "it just makes things that much harder." He made his way over to the concrete, followed closely by the Playleader. "Step aside," Straker called. He mounted to the top of the pile and surveyed the twenty children and one adult beneath him. He made a strange figure against the summer sky: a leprechaun-like little man dressed in long, black, velvet-lapelled jacket, high white shirt and black string tie, drainpipe tight trousers and dark-blue suede shoes with enormous crepe soles, the whole ensemble surmounted by a wolf-sharp and olive-complexioned grinning face under a mountainous pile of wavy, Brylcreemed hair. The children had never seen anything like it. The Playleader had; something was stirring dimly in the recesses of his memory.

"What's all that then?" shouted the boy called Facey. Straker took him to mean the concrete.

"It's gonna be a hut for you lot when I've finished wiv it," he told them.

The little ones cheered and danced about. The Playleader said sympathetically, "You're going to have a job shifting that lot about by yourself."

Straker said, "Yes I would, wouldn't I, by myself? You're going to have to help me, old son."

"Oh fuck *that*," scoffed the Playleader, who had an aversion to heavy work. There was a chorus of "Ooohs" and "Aaahs" and "dirty sods" from all around. "This can't be right," persisted the Playleader, his voice high with indignation. "Surely there should be enough workmen to put the thing up."

"Well there aint," said Straker coming down from the pile and standing squarely in front of the Playleader. "There's a shortage of skilled labour in London, you know, and here you are feeling the effects of it."

The Playleader scowled. Straker playfully tapped him. "Come on, old girl, it'll put hairs on that chest."

So all that day the Playleader stumbled to and fro with the sections of concrete, shamed by little Straker's tireless strength into (for him) prodigious feats of energy and endurance. By late afternoon he was sweaty, filthy, and ragged. Straker was unchanged, save for a somewhat brighter glistening of sweat and oil upon his forehead.

When the slabs were in place, flat down on the earth, the worst had passed. They had now to face the long and laborious task of fitting the sections together. But the terrible muscle-tearing lifting and carrying were behind them. They worked cordially together, stopping often for a smoke, and talking quietly, mostly about Straker's chequered life story.

"I've had a piss-poor time of it on the whole, haven't I?" he said gloomily after recounting one particularly disastrous episode. "I rue the fuckin day I was born sometimes."

The Playleader passed over another cigarette in silent sympathy. Straker took it, lit it, inhaled, exhaled mournfully. "Rue the fuckin day," he repeated.

"But you must have had *some* good times," urged the Playleader. Straker shook his head. But then smiled wistfully. "Well," he conceded, "there's been the one comfort." He looked shyly across at the Playleader. "The music. You know. The old Rock'n'Roll." His eyes flicked over the Playleader's shoulder-length hair. "I don't expect you know what I'm talking about," he said. "Ah but you don't know what you're missing, mate. I've lived for it. Chuck Berry, Fats, Bo Diddley! Fantastic!"

"I remember some of that stuff," the Playleader said brightly. "Chuck Berry and all that. I remember him."

Straker wasn't listening. "Ah but the greatest—*the* greatest— was Eddie Cochran." He looked over at the Playleader again. "I'm in his Club you know. We go on excursions and so on."

"I almost remember him," the Playleader said.

"He was fantastic. He was great. He died, you know. Killed in a car crash. Fantastic! And what was really something—his last tune, you know, in life—" Straker burst into song clicking his fingers to help himself along:

"'There are three steps to heaven
Listen and you will plainly see . . .'

Eddie's last song. 'Three Steps to Heaven'—and then bam! he dies. What d'you think of that? Weird isn't it? Frightening? Fantastic! The Club visits the hospital where he died every year, you know. It happened over here, you see."

They hefted a couple of concrete sections into place.

"I don't s'pose you can understand really," Straker said, sounding a little embarrassed now.

"No, I *do*," the Playleader promised. "I'm just old enough to remember all that stuff. And I remember too really liking it."

"*Liking* it!" scoffed Straker. "Anybody can *like* it." He leaned forward across the concrete. "But would you *die* for it?"

The Playleader shook his head, chastened.

"Well I would, nearly," Straker said, "if there was any point to it. It's bin me life, see. The best part of it anyway. Ever since down at the old Lewisham Odeon in 1956—*Rock around the Clock* and all that. Tearing up the seats, dancing in the aisles. The music. The clobber—" There was a catch in his voice. "—My life." He fell silent, and busied himself with his work.

The Playleader looked tenderly down at the emotional little man working hard at his side. "I really dig your luminous electric-green socks," he said kindly.

10

They knocked off at about six. The Playleader closed the Playground right away and started on his way home, leaving Straker to show his porno pictures to a knot of interested children outside the closed gate.

Before he was out of the park Straker had caught him up.

"Sell anything?" the Playleader asked.

Straker shook his head. "Nah. Well . . . A couple. Couldn't get more than five bob out of the little buggers. Never mind. It's always a pleasure doing business wiv kids. Being in their company and so on. Don't you find it so?" He looked up at the Playleader. "But you would naturally wiv a job like yours."

"Well, I don't know . . ." The Playleader always tried to be honest. "They're all right, you know, at a distance . . . I suppose they're all right. I never know what to say to em."

"Aaah, they like you."

"D'you think so?"

"Course they do. You can tell. I could *feel* it as soon as I come in. Believe me. I know kids. I can *tell*."

"You've got some of your own?"

Straker laughed, rubbed his nose. "Oh no. None actually of my own." He considered his reply. "But I'm very *fond* of em."

Straker suggested a cup of tea and "meet the boys". The Playleader, flattered, acquiesced. They crossed the housing estate—"Herbert Morrison Buildings"—and drove into a maze of little streets behind it. Straker bounded energetically along the pavement. The Playleader proceeded more slowly, out of habit checking through the windows of the houses with "For Sale" signs at their gates. Straker saw him at it. "Don't waste your time, mate," he called. "They're rubbish. Diabolical."

"Could be done up," the Playleader murmured automatically.

They arrived at a little café set at the end of one of the terraced rows. It was called simply "Rube's". The big window up front was steamed up. Through the vent came a dim roar of music. Straker, who now had a slightly apprehensive look on his face, caught the Playleader's arm. "Now," he said, "you'll like the boys. Very much. But, well . . . give em a moment or two to get used to you. Eh?"

They went inside. The air was thick and heavy with the fumes of cooking fat. Behind a low counter at the rear of the room, a little old lady shuffled between a tea urn and a plastic cake-cover which presently held three cup-cakes and a sausage roll. "Hi Rube," Straker called. She coughed over her fag and nodded back. "That's Rube," he told the Playleader. There were three tables in the room, two of them pushed together beside the blaring juke-box. Straker led the Playleader over to them. Three men sitting there regarded the Playleader with suspicious eyes.

"What you got there then, Strake?" one of them called above the music. He was big and burly under a worn suit of the same style but not the same quality as Straker's.

"Bloke I'm working wiv, Frank," Straker told him. "Exceptionally nice fella."

"Oh yeah?" Frank said, not warmly.

"Bit of a Chuck Berry fan," Straker said slyly. "I expect you'll have, you know, quite a lot to talk about."

"Chuck Berry, eh?" Frank looked the Playleader up and down. He leaned forward suddenly and announced, "I've met 'im, you know."

"Wow!" the Playleader said, genuinely impressed.

"That's right." Frank leaned back complacently in his chair.

From behind the counter the old lady called out, "Are you two wantin anything or can I rest up my feet?" Straker pressed the Playleader down in a chair opposite Frank.

"What would you like to have, my son? We drink coke here mostly. But there's tea too. Have a coke, will you? That's it. You sit tight and talk to Frank."

The Playleader, deserted, sat on the edge of his seat. Avoiding Frank's steady gaze, he stared at the walls around him which were covered with scores of fading publicity photos, many of them signed. The Playleader recognised a few. There was Elvis. There were Bill Haley and the Comets. There was Little Richard. Tucked up far away and rather small in one corner was a tiny and very early Cliff Richard. But most of the photos were unknown to the Playleader and the names mysterious. Who was Preston Epps? Freddy Bell? Dave Apple? Clyde McPhatter? The Cadillacs???

"Fair old collection eh?" Frank's voice cut in. Now his gaze seemed more friendly. "I doubt if there's another one like it. Outside the museums."

"It's really something," enthused the Playleader.

"Yeah'n Frank's met mosta them an all," one of the men flanking Frank said suddenly. "Haven't yer Frank?"

"'S'right man," Frank agreed. He plucked one of the photos off the wall. Beneath the smiling blond head in the picture was the inscription "To a good old boy, Frank Farrell, from a real friend."

"Jerry Lee Lewis," Frank intoned. He looked lovingly down at the photo. Then replaced it on the wall. "I got that standin fifteen hours outside the theatre he was in," he told the Playleader. "Not from his first visit though, I have to admit." His face darkened. He looked across the table scowling. "Of course *you* wouldn't know anythin about *that*."

The Playleader jerked upright, considered, remembered: "They kicked him out? Because his wife was only fourteen?"

"Thirteen," Frank corrected. "But you're right in essentials."

"I remember that well," the Playleader said eagerly, "because I was delivering newspapers at the time and I remember reading about it." He glanced shyly at the three men opposite. "It seemed a tough deal," he ventured.

"It was *infamous*," Frank snarled, squeezing in his anger the plastic ketchup bottle before him. "She was *fully* mature." A little bit of red sauce wriggled out of the hole. Alertly one of the men next to Frank scooped it up and licked his finger heartily.

"Gotta passion for the stuff," he confided to the Playleader.

Straker was back, plonking a couple of warm cokes down on the table, and squeezing the Playleader's shoulder in a motherly way. "Gettin on all right are you?" he fussed. "Here's your coke, and here's your straw, and here—here's a nice cigarette too in your mouth." He settled down beside the Playleader. "That's right," he said comfortably. "Now. What's new?" he asked the other side of the table generally.

"I'm all right, Strake," mumbled the man on Frank's left.

"Are you Gordon? Good. And Terry?"

"All right, Strake. Not too bad, I s'pose," said the man on Frank's right. "How's yourself?"

"Well . . ." Straker pulled deeply on his straw. "Me and er—" He nodded at the Playleader, "—have had a pretty hard day of it really, haven't we? Down at this playground."

"Workin in a playground, Strake?" Terry guffawed. "Talk about cat among the fuckin pigeons!"

Straker regarded the man coldly. Then turned to Frank. "You OK are you, Frankie?" he asked in an oddly gentle and coaxing voice.

Thus cossetted, Frank gave a little wry smile and shook his head. "Not so good today," he said, working his shoulder and wincing as he did so. "We had to clear out two whole bays. Shockin rough on the old hands."

He held them out in proof. The Playleader gasped to see them. They were horribly torn and battered, a mass of old scar tissue. There were new wounds in them too. As Frank flexed them painfully, fresh blood oozed along the grey creases of his palms. He laughed to see the Playleader's appalled face. "I'm a *real* working-man," he told him playfully.

Straker's lips were thin and tight. He said crisply, with a relevance that was obviously clear to everyone else around the table but which the Playleader couldn't fathom, "I saw Artie Riley yesterday night, Frank."

"Oh, did yer," grunted Frank, scowling.

"Yes I did. He asked after you. He wants to see you."

"Well, I don' care to see 'im."

"He wants to *help* you, Frank."

"I don' need it. Did yer tell 'im that?"

"Yeah, I told 'im," Straker flashed angrily. "I told 'im you liked livin and workin like a fuckin pig an all."

"That's right," Frank almost shouted, "I *do*." The two men glared at each other savagely.

Alarmed by this mysterious quarrel, the Playleader was relieved to hear behind him the ping of the café door opening.

"It's yer tart, Frank," Gordon said. He stood up to let a woman of about thirty-one, thirty-two sit down at Frank's side. She wore a duffel coat and her fair hair was tied up in a pony-tail, a look that had such associations of adolescent youthfulness for the Playleader that it was oddly disturbing to look at the comfortable, early middle-aged face of the woman opposite. However, he smiled tentatively in greeting, hoping to create another ally in her.

"What you brought in there, Strake?" she asked nastily as soon as she had settled in. "New boy friend?"

"Bloke works wiv me," Straker said sullenly.

The woman regarded the Playleader with hard eyes, then put her arm in Frank's. "Didn't know you was lettin fuckin 'ippies in 'ere Frank," she sighed in his ear, her eyes flicking across at the Playleader who touched his long hair nervously.

"Shocking little stirrer is Isobel," said Straker to the Playleader. "Ignore her."

The woman released Frank and turned to Gordon. "You haven't gone soft on me like Frank, have you?" she murmured. "You aint gonna let a fuckin 'ippie bovver us?"

Gordon shuffled in his seat and looked across at Frank for directions.

"No violence please," Straker implored. "Frank . . . a Chuck Berry fan . . . Please Frank!"

Frank thought the matter over, fiddling with a salt-and-pepper shaker all the while. Then he looked across at the shrinking Playleader. "See," Frank told him mildly. "We been coming into Rube's for . . . what?" He looked around for help, worked it out himself. "Fourteen, fifteen years." He paused, startled at the thought. Then resumed hesitatingly "See. It's nothin personal. But this is all we got. If we let one of you in, you'd be all over us, wouldn't you?"

"It's like wiv the niggers," Gordon put in helpfully.

Frank nodded. "That's right," he said. "You understand, don't you? We've put a lot into this place. A lot of time and graft. All them pictures. And the records. We got early Dell-Vikings for instance, and all of Frankie Lymon. Who'd look after em if we was gone? Nobody. So we can't risk anythin, see? So we gotta rule here. No strangers."

The Playleader half rose. "I do understand," he trembled. "I'm so sorry I'm here. I'll be off now."

"He don't get away that easy, does he, Frank," the dreadful woman sniggered. Frank looked down at his enormous butchered fists, and then speculatively up at the Playleader. Everything, even the juke-box, was silent. Then "Go on," Frank ordered abruptly. "Hoppit. Scarper."

The Playleader was out of the door in a flash, cutting off the woman's cry of frustration as he slammed it behind him. As he twinkled down the road, he heard Straker's voice calling him from behind. But he only quickened his pace, and didn't look round or pause for breath until he had reached the park railings, home and safe.

II

STRAKER APOLOGISED TO him the next day in the Playground. "I wish it had turned out different," he said. "I had hopes. I reckon we need new blood down at Rube's."

"That fucking woman!" the Playleader shuddered.

"Isobel?" said Straker reflectively. "And yet a nice bird on the whole. Just this one weakness. She loves the violence. She's a stirrer."

Straker went off by himself to finish up the hut. The Playleader gently patrolled his playground, and inspected its inhabitants. He was learning at last, in a spotty sort of way, to distinguish faces and attach names to them. There were Denis and Harmon and their friends of course. Without knowing very much about any of them, he enjoyed genial relationships with them all, particularly on their joint paydays. But he was also becoming aware of less-obtrusive folk. Such as, for instance, Gary, a little kid with freckles, a whiz on the tarzan rope, and Marlene, six years old and incredibly pretty, who spent her days obsessively making mud pies behind the hill, accompanied only by a black kid, about the same age, West African by the tribal markings, who watched her intensely, applauded specially good pies, and hissed the failures. Marlene ignored him entirely. Then there were a couple of small boys from the short row of vast Victorian houses that lined the base of the park. They both wore turtle-neck sweaters and corduroy shorts. Their straw-coloured hair hung low over their ears and down the backs of their necks. They were called Piers and Blaise, and from the first the Playleader couldn't help his middle-class heart going out to them. They arrived one morning together, marched smartly up to him, and Blaise—the older at about ten—introduced himself and Piers and then, after a lightning move from the cluster of kids who had gathered to observe them, announced "That boy just hit me." He looked hopefully up at the Playleader who could only offer him a comradely shrug. For the first day Blaise and Piers hung round the Playleader peppering him with information about their school (in Sussex), their holidays (Norway), and their accountant Daddy and doctor Mummy. All the time they were watching the Play-ground with wary eyes, fixing in their minds the location of the safe open spaces and of the dangerous corners, checking each exit, picking out the likely sources of peril among the other children, and generally testing the temperature of the water. On the next day they ventured gingerly in. The Playleader saw here and there a spiteful tug at their long hair, a kick aimed at their natty shorts. But they were quite tough little boys and though nobody—except Gloria, who soon and rather obstreperously showed that she fan-cied Blaise—particularly befriended them, they seemed, after a few days, to be surviving reasonably happily.

With Gloria's friend the Playleader's relationship grew quite idyllic. She was seldom out of his company, she made sure he was never out of her sight. This monopolising led to some harsh words between her and Blaise and Piers during the latters' first day in the Playground. Yet it was only of her contemporaries that she seemed to be jealous. She often asked after Alice and was eager to hear what she did, how she looked, how she dressed, where they had met, whether she would ever come down to visit the Playground. Once she brought for Alice a tiny cellophane packet of ladies handkerchiefs. She had found them at the bottom of her mother's

dressing table. She said they were probably just an unwanted present from some Christmas or birthday and "Go on, take em. My
mum never blows her nose." She lived with her mother over in the
Herbert Morrison Buildings. Her father had left the home when
she was a baby.

The Playleader, though nervous of her as of any child, liked
her too and admired and enjoyed her steadfast devotion to him.
Absurdly, he still did not know her name and spent much time
thinking of ways to discover it without hurting her by revealing
his ignorance. He was reluctant to ask any of the other kids for
fear that it might get back to her. And so all he could do was to
hope that someone would call out her name in his presence. But it
had not happened yet. Her attachment to him was exclusive. She
was content in her monogamy. She shut out all others, and they
avoided her.

So the Playleader strolled across his turf, able to pick out here
and there, much more often than he would have imagined, familiar friendly faces. It was a perfect day—hot and dry. The children
were out in numbers and responding to the sunshine. It was noisy
but good-tempered. There was none of the awful cacophony of
the first week, no frightened shrieks, angry curses, brutal bashings
in odd corners. Wandering hither and thither, calling out the occa-
sional greeting to this and that clump of happy children, ponder-
ing the power of sunshine and of Tenby's ten quid, the Playleader
felt enchanted with his place and position, seeing himself as the
much-loved monarch of a peaceable kingdom where truly it might
be said that the lions lay down with the lambs.

Behind the now-finished concrete hut, he came upon Straker
lying down with a black kid of about twelve, his mouth pressed to
the open flies of the child's jeans. He rose reluctantly at the Playleader's approach. The boy too got to his feet, smiling cheerfully.

"That bloke's fuckin bent," he said to the Playleader, jerking a
thumb at Straker who was slowly getting into his drape jacket. Then
he accepted a fifty pence piece from Straker and, winking at the
Playleader, ran whooping off to join the queue for the tarzan rope.

The Playleader didn't know what to say. "No harm done,"
Straker assured him, "is there?"

The Playleader looked at the hut, admired its professional finish. "You'll be off now," he stated.

"See," explained Straker, "I never done it wiv a little sambo before."

The Playleader accompanied him to the gate. Straker was despondent.

"Seems a shame," he said, "after we got on so well." He handed the Playleader a cigarette, took one himself, and lit them both. Then he leaned against the gate, gazing mournfully into the Playground. In the late, dying sun the slim forms of the youths on the ropes made long and looping shadows as they swung under the trees. The sadness dropped from Straker's eyes as he watched the flying boys. A look of gentle lust replaced it. Finally he faced the Playleader and grinned. "Fuckin Garden of Eden you got in there!" he cried. "Look after it, for Gawd's sake!" Then they shook hands and Straker swung jauntily off down the lane.

Part Two

I

ONE EVENING, ABOUT ten o'clock, at the end of the Playleader's third week of work, Alice, his wife, telephoned him at home. Her voice was dreamy; she sounded stoned. "Come over, love," she said. "And drive me home." A pause for thought. "And meet someone nice."

Judging by that pause, the Playleader thought, it looked to be a depressingly momentous occasion ahead. To hell with her denials. He simply could not avoid the obvious conclusion that the evidence of Alice's late nights, irritability, and non-fucking (with him) was pointing to. He prepared to meet her lover.

Driving down the King's Road in their dusty Mini he thought glumly of the ordeal ahead. He had no idea how he would carry it off. He hoped deeply he would not shame Alice. It depended very much, he thought, on whether they wanted to admit their relationship to him out loud. Or would they stay silent, leaving him to guess? One of these courses would be disastrous for him, he feared. He was not sure which.

Of course, he was not afraid of losing Alice. He was too absolutely dependent on her for her to consider that. She had humanity in her, a great deal of it. So there was no fear of actual desertion. Nothing as bad as that.

Still, this was the first time that Alice had availed herself of the rules by which they had first promised to live their married life. (He could not, in fact, remember whether those rules permitted actual introductions to one's lovers. Wasn't there a vow of secrecy in them somewhere?) Like everybody they knew, they had believed as a matter of course that outside affairs were permissible, possibly even necessary, in a healthy marriage. So before their wedding they had plotted calmly and confidently to circumscribe and render harmless these future liaisons by, for instance, laying it down that they should not involve any of their friends and, most importantly, that they should contain in them, as far as possible, only sex, none of the emotion that belonged properly to their marriage. They were not, in fact, really entirely clear why they had actually got married at all. There were the parents of course; certain financial inducements; it was all very weak of them. But having agreed to do the deed, it seemed to them that their rules, loyally obeyed, might at least help them to avoid the odious marital fuck-ups of the generations ahead of them.

The Playleader remembered now with a pang that it was he who had been most insistent about the need for rules. For they were then largely for his convenience, some way to contain his rampant and extraordinarily successful screwing around within the framework of Alice and himself and marriage. Those were brave times. For him. Even in—well, especially in—his present wiped-out condition, he liked to look back on them, when the prosperous unfolding of his life seemed to communicate itself in some strange intense sexual fashion to the women, the many women, the yards and yards of cunt that measured out those juicy days. Then he had held tight in his hand a bag of goodies that bulged far out in all the right directions—the career, the money, Alice the adoring wife, the many merry mistresses, and health, hope, happiness, sound politics, and good, sane thoughts. In those happy days he was at the fine peak of his trajectory—and so blissfully unaware it already had levelled onto a narrow plateau.

Tonight Alice was up to whatever she was over in Islington. It was an up-and-coming district. The Playleader drove into a warren of treeless streets, the huddled terraced houses on either side divided about equally between traditional unkempt and an assortment of freshly done-up frontages in cream, or greeny khaki, or cloud blue, the latter type very often with a little pile of new bricks in their tiny front yards.

At the house which held his wife the front-door chimes played a little tune as he pressed the button. It was something more than vaguely familiar. The Playleader rang the chimes again to jog his memory. As the notes died away the door was opened by a tall, good-looking young man.

"It's the start of 'As Time Goes By'," he told the Playleader help-fully. "From *Casablanca*."

"Thank you," said the Playleader, nervously polite.

"I'm Jonathan Ames," the other said. "Come in."

In the large living room—two rooms knocked into one—Alice was lying on a sofa, her eyes closed. The Playleader sniffed a famil-iar aroma.

"I'm sorry it's all gone," Jonathan apologised. "I only had a little."

The Playleader touched his wife's arm. She opened her eyes and focused dreamily up at him. She smiled tenderly.

"Oh, I'm *so* glad you're here," she murmured. "But you missed some such good stuff."

Jonathan was moving round the room, knocking out ashtrays, picking up glasses, putting books back into the cream shelves that lined one wall. Alice rolled over on the sofa. "I'm starving," she said.

"We'll go out?" Jonathan asked, looking over at the Playleader, who found it hard to meet his eyes.

"I want something nice and sweet and sticky," Alice announced in a little girl voice.

"I know where you can get thick milk shakes near here," Jona-than said.

"*That's* what I want," Alice smiled up at the two men. "I *must* have a milk shake."

In the Mini the front seat was made crowded by Jonathan's gor-geous fur coat. "Sorry about this," he apologised to the Playleader, "I'm abnormally affected by cold."

Alice sprawled in the back, draping her arms over the two up front. "You know," she said in the Playleader's ear, "Jonathan got that *fantastic* coat entirely on his expenses money. *Fifty* quid."

"Well, you see, I'm at the BBC," Jonathan explained to the Play-leader.

"You know that programme we watched, my man the poet was on, you *know*, the panel game? Jonathan's on that. That's how I know him." They bumped along in the little car, turning right at an intersection at Jonathan's direction. "Show him your wad, Jona-than," Alice urged.

Jonathan laughed shyly.

"Come on," said Alice, "he'd love to see it."

"Well," said Jonathan apologetically to the Playleader. "You know how they are down there at the Beeb over money. Quite ridiculous. No control at all." He produced from his fur coat a thick stack of five and one pound notes and riffled through them under the Playleader's eyes. It was impressive certainly.

"There's about a hundred and twenty quid there," Alice said excitedly. "All expenses. Just as a float. What do you think of that?"

"You must have a pretty high-up job there," the Playleader said, humble in spite of himself.

Jonathan seemed very faintly embarrassed. "Well, no, actually," he said. "Just a researcher, in fact. My *God*! You should *see* the bread the *producers* are putting away! Cars they're buying. Yachts already! Christ!"

The Playleader thought bitterly of his TV licence fee. Then he thought more bitterly about being cuckolded. "It's a shitty show," he said. "That panel game. The one you're on."

"It *is* shitty, isn't it," nodded Jonathan. "I despise it. Never mind. It won't be renewed."

They arrived at the restaurant. Alice had fallen asleep. They woke her and, both propping her up, walked her in. Jonathan ordered a double-hamburger with American cheese but without the french fries, and a coke; Alice had a deep-dish apple pie with a double-dab of ice cream and a strawberry milk shake; the Playleader had a cup of black coffee. Conversation was not easy. A bad rock band was on the stereo at deafening volume, thin boy waiters in tee shirts and flared Levis continually bumped into and off their table, marshalling customers into their seats, through their snacks, and finally out through the swing doors again. Alice kept falling asleep. The two men communicated in abrupt roars, spending most of their time gazing at the big pretty girl who lolled in the chair between them.

Jonathan asked after playleading. The Playleader said it was all right, how was the BBC? Uphill, Jonathan told him. After propping up Alice to eat her apple pie, they talked politics. It had been a violent week on the News. Jonathan was firm and committed and passionate. The Playleader, it soon developed, didn't really understand the issues at stake. In a clear patrician voice, Jonathan patiently elucidated them. The Playleader found himself warming to this boy friend of his wife who was taking so much trouble over educating him. He bellowed his thanks across the table.

Alice, woken by the noise, looked trustingly from face to face. "I knew you two would get on," she told them. Jonathan tenderly wiped a morsel of ice cream from the corner of her mouth. Leaning over the table to do this, his head came under the light. The Playleader saw that he was even more good-looking than he had first thought. But not blandly so, his smooth English face was enriched by a fine big beak of a nose, and framed in a mass of tight dark curls. The Playleader was glad in a way that his wife had such an attractive lover; it re-inforced her worth to him. Besides, he simply wished her well. He felt now that he could adjust to this situation. Perhaps Jonathan could even be a friend for both of them. He smiled across the table at his companions. Alice smiled affectionately back. But Jonathan was snapping at his cheeseburger and didn't see the Playleader's little effort.

When they had finished their meal, they tried to sit for a while enjoying the shared harmony. But the bad music and an officious waiter drove them out. The Playleader handsomely paid up for the whole bill. In the street outside Jonathan offered to take a taxi home. The Playleader wouldn't hear of it. Exhilarated by now at the civilised way the situation was developing, he enthusiastically bore Jonathan back to Islington in the Mini. There were loving three-way goodbyes at the curb-side outside Jonathan's nice little house. Then husband and wife made the long drive home in comfortable silence, she dozing sometimes on his shoulder.

In bed they held each other close. "Well," said the Playleader, "it's a relief to know."

"To know what?" Alice asked curiously.

The Playleader massaged her nipple while she murmured happily. "Come on," he said, "you can say the words."

"What words?" she asked, a mite irritated.

"About . . . Jonathan, of course. Oh come on. Look at me. See, I'm not upset at all."

She was silent. And then she laughed.

"Come on," he repeated, "I know he's the one."

She propped herself up and kissed his forehead. "You don't know anything at all, sweet pea," she said firmly. She laughed again and, with womanly gallantry, tickled his balls.

"Alice!" he appealed, wriggling under her touch, "be fair. Late at the office every night. No sex. Bad temper. You can't fool me."

She eased herself on top of him, tucking him inside of her. In his ear she gave a silly stoned giggle. "Come down Alice's rabbit hole," she whispered.

Perplexed, he asked, almost disappointed, "Isn't it Jonathan then?"

"Oh no!" she sighed happily, moving upon him. "Not him at all."

"Really not?"

She brought his head against her breast. "Would I lie?" she breathed. "Believe me. There's no other man. Poor thing. No other man than you. Cross my heart and hope to die!"

So then they had a marvellous time. The Playleader stayed inside for fifty minutes and Alice came three times. But in the morning she was cool again, and acted embarrassed and irritated with him, as bad as ever. He didn't know what to think.

2

TENBY PAID A visit to the Playground a couple of days later. The Playleader had been taking the sun in a favourite corner, propped up against a log, with Gloria's friend nearby, lying on her stomach reading a comic. From this position he watched Tenby crossing the Playground, picking his way with evident distaste through the fast-moving knots of children. It was another hot day in this marvellous summer, and Tenby's plump face was as pink as his shirt. The Playleader struggled to his feet.

"So you're still here?" Tenby called. He came up close and shook the Playleader's hand. "We figured when we didn't hear from you that something bad must have happened." He looked around the Playground, wiping the sweat off his forehead with a paisley handkerchief. "Looks OK," he nodded appreciatively. "No blood anyway."

They set off on a tour of the Playground, trailed closely by Gloria's friend.

"I'm sorry I haven't shown my face earlier," Tenby said. "I've been *brutally* busy with my new book, you see." He glanced across at the Playleader, who looked suitably impressed. "It's rather a super production," Tenby continued. "All sort of to do with children's play and violence on TV and connections therein. In fact, I'm collaborating with a rather well-known television producer." He mentioned Jonathan's name. "Do you know his work?"

The Playleader was amused at the coincidence. "Why, I know *him*," he said, "but I thought he was just a researcher?"

"A nice guy, Jonathan," Tenby nodded. "Incurably modest. We're having enormous fun together. The book's shaping very well. That reminds me." He stopped and looked keenly about. "I must remember to talk to a couple of kids here before I go. If you could dig up one or two who are reasonably, you know, in control of themselves I'd be so grateful. We're going to have original research you see. And illustrations. We have fantastic hopes for it. It'll do us both a lot of good. We *practically* have a publisher. We have an in, you see." He chortled. "Well, I should say *Jonathan* has an in. He's screwing the knickers off this bird who works in a publisher's, you know, and she almost *guarantees* acceptance."

The Playleader felt a sad twinge, but gamely kept up with the other's long strides.

"Hut looks smashing," Tenby admired, stopping before it. "The kids have made a filthy mess of it though."

"I think it's nice that they painted it themselves."

"I dare say." Tenby shook his head. "Theoretically, I dare say. But it looks quite vile."

They took another diagonal across the Playground. As they passed Denis's lemon-yellow and pink shack, Ivor Norton, one of his mates, wriggled out, dragging with him two large paper bags which gave out the musical clink of glass on glass. "Takin in the empties," he announced to the two men as he passed.

Tenby watched him go. Ivor at fifteen-and-a-half was six foot three and well-muscled. "Christ. How do you handle them that size?" he asked wonderingly.

"Magic!" said the Playleader.

They came upon three boys fighting; one of them was Blaise. They were all very small and the Playleader waded in without hesitation, kicking and cuffing and finally separating them. The three ran away and hid in a tree, from whence Blaise's voice could be heard fluting "Rotten swine!" down at the Playleader. It had been a thoroughly successful engagement. The Playleader was only lightly sweating. Tenby, admiring, handed him a cigarette.

"You have the *knack*," he said. "You run a tight Playground." He looked the Playleader over appraisingly. "And you're quite clean too." He thought for a moment, then asked, "What are you going to do this winter when the Playground closes?"

"Dunno. Factory perhaps."

"Have you got a degree? No? What have you got? . . . Oh. Well. That's about the same, isn't it." Tenby hesitated. "And after all," he said slowly, "you have natural ability and that's what counts, not all this book-learning crap. Right?"

"What's all this about?" asked the Playleader.

"Well," said Tenby, all in a rush, "there's this lectureship thing at this university, you see. It's a new post. Lecturing in playleading—or in fact Recreational Science, it's called. Should be fascinating. I don't suppose *you'd* fancy it?"

"Me? *No*. Christ!"

Tenby nodded energetically. "I *know*. I do *understand*. It's an incredibly humiliating thing to have to ask you. But . . . well, it would help us all out a fantastic lot. We have this grant to spend, you see, and it all rather revolves around finding some warm body to fill this fucking university job. Harrison's put me on to finding someone. Really I don't think it would be *too* tough. I mean there wouldn't be anything much to do. Lecture a bit, I suppose. Do a book maybe . . . and you'd have students to write that of course. Attend a sherry party perhaps."

"*No*," repeated the Playleader firmly, "I can't. Not possibly. You

know . . . I've come down pretty far but. . . ." There was a catch in
his voice.

Tenby nodded again. "We'll say no more about it," he said sympathetically. "I'm sorry I brought it up. We're just that desperate.
I mean"—he stared at the Playleader tragically—"knowing Harrison, it may even mean *I* have to do the bloody thing."

They wandered sombrely towards the gate. The Playleader
stopped before they reached it. "You wanted two kids to interview
for your book," he reminded Tenby.

The other gave a final disgusted look around the seething Playground, then clapped the Playleader on his shoulder. "I'll make
it up, old boy. It'll come out so much better that way. It does for
everybody else, anyway."

3

EVERYBODY AGREED WITH Tenby in liking the new hut. Even the
Park-keeper, gazing at it suspiciously from across the fence, gave
it a grudging tribute (though he did think there should have been
separate facilities for the blacks). "I wish to Christ I lived anywhere
half as good," he snarled.

The kids were completely delighted with it, many of them
spending entire days, even during the brightest, hottest weather, in
the dark roomy interior, painting the walls and setting up posters.
When it rained, everyone turned up at the Playground to cram
inside the hut. The crush of damp bodies and the warm steam
rising got a little headachy. But it was undeniably cosy.

The hut's fame spread. People from the neighbourhood came
down to watch their children climbing all over its roof, wield-
ing brushes and laying down coat upon coat of bright, primary-
coloured paint. Several braved the "No Adults allowed in Here"
notice at the Playground gate and came in to poke around inside
the hut. One pair of fathers even took over the ping-pong table for
a couple of hours, causing the Playleader, who was far too nervous
to tell them off, much anxiety and a certain drop in prestige among
the angry children who vainly ordered him to intervene.

So, coming in the hut late one afternoon, the Playleader was not too surprised to find a youngish middle-aged man—thick-set, wearing a dark-blue, well-cut suit—looking around in the back of the room. He was accompanied by Denis Riley.

"My dad," Denis explained, jerking a thumb at the man. And then, jerking the thumb at the Playleader, told his father, "The bloke I told you about who's in charge here."

The Playleader was touched that tough Denis would bring his father to see him. "Pleased to meet you," he said cordially, holding out his hand. Denis's father took it, considered it, then firmly shook it.

"Right," he said. "Right." Then he turned away to look around the back of the room some more.

"What d'you think, dad?" Denis asked anxiously.

His father ignored him, asking the Playleader, "You lock this place every night?" He had a soft Irish accent.

"Oh yes," said the Playleader brightly, "every night."

"Anybody snoop around here? Park-keepers or anything?"

"Nah," said Denis. "There's only 'im. He's the only one around regular. Fairy bloke in a pink shirt comes in once in a while. But he don't stay long, does he?"

The Playleader figured out that Denis meant Tenby and shook his head.

Denis's father seemed to come to a decision. He took the Playleader by the elbow and drew him into the shadowy rear of the hut. "I'll tell you what it is," he said, quickly and quietly. "I want to be able to drop a few business things off here once in a while. Just drop stuff here, see? Leave it here and then pick it up again. All right?"

The Playleader didn't really follow him. "Well, hell, you know . . ." he stumbled, hurting a little under the big man's grip, "this is Recreation Department property after all. I'm not sure if I *can* store things here. I mean, there's all the kids' stuff to set up here. I've invoiced for a miniature billiard table for instance. We haven't really got the room, you see . . . What kind of stuff?"

Denis's father said, "Bits and pieces. It would vary. You know. Sometimes something very simple. A TV set or something. Sometimes maybe something like a little parcel or a packet of something. Another time a record player. You know."

"Are they hot?" asked the Playleader knowingly.

Denis's father winked at him. "Might of fallen off the back," he agreed.

The Playleader considered. It was all rather exciting really. "There wouldn't be anything very *big*?" he asked. "Oh nothing *big*," assured the father. "And," his voice dropped a decibel, "there'd be something in it for you."

"What?" whispered the Playleader.

"Ten pound a week if you can keep your hands off the stuff. And I'll chop em off at the wrist if you can't." The father's eyes glittered in the gloom. "Money for old rope," he urged. "Will you do it?"

The Playleader, somewhat numbed by this excessive threat, nodded assent. That evening Denis's father arrived at the hut laden with two tape recorders and a brown paper parcel. He stored them all under a tarpaulin at the back of the hut. Before leaving he slipped two fivers into the Playleader's outstretched hand. However, the following day first Denis and then Harmon upped their protection charges by two pounds each, and so the Playleader was only able to hold on to six.

4

ALICE BROUGHT HOME a treat for her husband a couple of days later. The Playleader was relaxing in the bath tub at the time. Piers had had a birthday party that afternoon in the Playground, and it had turned into a bit of a brawl. The little girl Marlene had thrown up, and Gloria's friend had gone into a tantrum over the Playleader's attempt to comfort her. And so now he was glad to lie in the warm soapy water, letting the dust and the heat and the trouble of the day tumble away from him.

His eyes were closed when Alice and the strange lady appeared at the bathroom door. "Well . . . there he is," he heard his wife say. Looking up and beyond Alice, who was wearing her now custom-

ary faintly peeved expression, he saw a cool, sallow, angular face
staring down at him.

"This is Portia," Alice told him.

The Playleader risked a peep down at his genitals and was
relieved to see they were doing nothing out of the way, just float-
ing there. It would be gauche, he decided, to cover them up.

"Hello Portia," he called.

"Hi," she said laconically, turning away. "I could use some
coffee, Alice."

The Playleader listened to them clattering about in the kitchen.
He heard Alice laugh twice; Portia seemed to be doing most of the
talking. He examined critically his sloping abdomen which lay just
below the water; pressing down on it with his finger tips, he suspected himself of a slight swelling paunch. He heard Alice laugh
again. The water was cooling rapidly now and goose-pimples were
forming on his arms. He tried to remember as he rose from the
tub if he had heard of a Portia among Alice's friends before. He
thought not.

He dressed carefully in fresh undies, an illustrated T-shirt, and
scarlet jeans, keen to make a good impression on Alice's new pal.
(And what a lot of new pals she'd been collecting lately, he marvelled to himself.) But definitely he felt put in the shade by Portia's
ensemble which was fully revealed to him when he joined them in
the kitchen. She was all in black—combat jacket, T-shirt, leather
pants and motor-cycle boots, all a gritty black. Around her neck
she had slung two leather ropes, from one of which dangled a
heavy metal peace sign, and from the other a wooden swastika.
From her shoulder hung a Nikon camera. On one arm of her
combat jacket she had sewn sergeant's stripes, on the other miniature United States and Danish flags. And when she turned her
back—which she did at the Playleader's entrance—he could read
in studs upon her jacket the legend "East Oakland Bikers Club.
Death Before Dishonour."

The Playleader, knocked out by her outfit, was sorry she had
turned away from him. Had he offended her already? Alice too,
he saw with regret, seemed to be looking at him with more than
usual irritation.

"Um, Portia. . . ." he stumbled.

She turned round, holding in her hand a mug of coffee which she handed to him. "I poured you this," she said, looking steadily into his eyes. "It's good and hot."

The Playleader took the coffee and sat down on a high stool, sipping the drink and gazing respectfully at this remarkable woman. He wondered how old she was. In her thirties possibly, he thought.

Portia laughed suddenly. She looked at Alice and said, "I think your hubby's curious about me."

Alice tossed her head impatiently.

"What a minx she is to be sure," Portia said, turning round to smile in an oddly comradely fashion at the Playleader. Then Alice smiled too, stood up, and came across the room and tickled the Playleader's scalp.

"Is *she* doing a book for you too?" he asked her.

"No," Alice said. "Although she *should*, the cow! She's from Women's Lib."

"In a manner of speaking," Portia said. Alice giggled mysteriously.

"You're American," the Playleader stated.

"Right," said Portia. "San Francisco mainly."

"She's a journalist," said Alice. "Aren't you?"

"What do you write about," asked the Playleader. "What's your beat?"

"What's my beat?" said Portia to the empty air.

"She writes about herself," said Alice, stroking his hair. "Don't you Portia? And just her life and what's happening and who she meets and where she goes. A constant flow."

"I'd like to read that," said the Playleader.

Portia scuffled in the large, leather, cigarette-burned bag she had hung from the arm of her chair. "You can," she said. She brought out a thick crumpled newspaper and handed it over. The Playleader riffled through it. It seemed to be composed mostly of ads for water beds at $99.95.

"Portia's on page ten," Alice told him. The Playleader found it: "Seximental Journey" by Portia Epstein. Dateline London.

So that was paris (he read) and who knows what the fuck F is
doing now? or who? and who cares anyway? not me london
now is something else a motherfuckin huge giant of a shitty
tis pity she's a whore city. Monetary crisis and lilac blossoms
are heavy in the air as I pace randy up and down piccadilly
street the people passing by gawping at me gawp gawp this
bunch of yo-yos empire-looser boob-makers extraordinary
. . . and there are some boobs here by the way I wouldn't
mind making *at all* heh heh! but shit the only thing that matters in this shitty city is to think that somewhere J and Y are
here too somewhere in white perhaps just around the corner
. . . tho frankly I'm waiting for *them* to call *me* first this time
for once and if yoko wants to forget the favours I did her
when she was fresh down from sarah lawrence just getting
started all right I'm not breaking my balls for her anymore
. . . whatever her predicament which granted is major. The
same, slightly less so goes for X . . . ah shit but I miss bunny
this british nite and josie who plays her lute so nice and M
who motor-sickled me Marin county across every nite one
summer which summer? under the far fucking far out stars.

The Playleader looked up bemused. "Who reads this stuff?" he
asked limply. "Who buys this paper?"

"Freaks, idiots, college professors," Portia said. "Don't knock it.
It's a genre." She recovered the newspaper and stuffed it back in
her bag, clearly a little put out by his reaction. But not too much.

"I'm going to get into it pretty soon," Alice told him excitedly.
"It *is* pretty soon isn't it, Portia?"

The older woman regarded the younger thoughtfully. "Yeah,
pretty soon," she said. "I air-mailed some copy Tuesday."

Portia stayed for supper, and at the other two's prompting
talked quite a bit about herself. She was over in Europe attending
conferences—"war, poverty, Women's Lib, all that *schtick*"—and
sometimes speaking from the platform. She'd just come back from
a Women's Lib seminar in Cambridge where she'd stayed in some
comfort at a young Newnham don's house. She fished out of her
bag to show them a couple of expensive little objects she had "lib-

erated" from the lady scholar's sideboard. She hadn't enjoyed the seminar, describing her fellow liberationists as having "no flair, no style, no balls". Most of them too had unliberated nannies and au pairs in the background taking care of the kids. And the town of Cambridge had been a disappointment as well. "Poky little place," she said. "Shitty-looking people."

She was spending most of her time in England just checking out people she'd run into previously in Rangoon or Los Angeles or Amsterdam or somewhere who were now, like her, passing through London. She scattered her conversation with many fairly famous names—writers, pop musicians, film people—and with one or two biggies, all people she had talked to, written to, written about, smoked with, lived with. Alice listened to it all with a rapt expression. And the Playleader too, groping after Portia's high speed narrative, enjoyed her thoroughly, soon forgiving her her habit of writing garbage.

"So," Portia said finally to the Playleader. "So what do *you* do."

Alice was clearly ashamed of him. "He's really just in between jobs at the moment. Aren't you?"

"I'm a playleader," he said with dignity.

"Playleader! What's that?" Portia asked.

Alice said, "It's so feeble really. He messes around with little children all day. That's all he does."

"I look after a Playground," he explained. "I—well, I open it in the morning, and . . . close it in the evening. And just sort of while away the time in between."

"Yeah, that does sound pretty feeble," Portia said. "Nevertheless," she thought for a moment, "my readers sometimes dig that kind of shit." She looked up quickly. "I don't mean that in any hypocritical kind of way. I just find kids very very boring."

"Me too," Alice said firmly.

"But a lot of people swear by them," Portia mused. "Maybe I could come down to this Playground and check it out. Could I do that?"

Alice pouted. "That means *he'll* be in your column too."

Portia leaned across laughing to touch the girl's arm. "He'll be in there anyway, hon," she said. "He can't hardly miss, can he?"

So, before Alice drove her home, Portia had fixed up a date to visit the Playground. When the women had gone, the Playleader cheerfully washed the stack of dirty dishes. He read two chapters of a novel and then, feeling tired, went to bed. Luckily he had not yet fallen asleep when the telephone rang. It was Alice to say that there were so many "fantastic people" in the flat Portia was staying in that she might be late home, well she might even stay all night, OK? The Playleader wished her well and, after one or two involuntary moody thoughts, fell fast asleep and slept till morning when he woke alone.

5

THAT SAME DAY in the afternoon the Playleader came back from a bite to eat at a nearby café—not Rube's—to find Straker standing just outside the gates to the Playground. The dapper little man came up with a nervous ingratiating smile and the Playleader, in spite of himself, felt glad to see him.

"I didn't go inside," Straker called. "Not once."

"That's all right," the Playleader said. "Come inside. Look how your hut's doing."

They walked in together, and Straker admired the many-coloured hut.

"It's nice," he said. "Nice and cheerful."

Gloria's friend popped out of the hut to set up a couple of chairs for them on the concrete front. They settled in them, smoking comfortably.

"What brings you round here?" the Playleader asked.

"Two things," Straker said. "First, I must deliver me orders." He patted his inside jacket pocket. "A couple of em are for you." He fished out two photographs. "Lady wiv the dog. And two ladies on the go in a bath." He handed them over. "I can't understand you fancying women doing it wiv each other," he said, a little censoriously.

The Playleader was happily studying the picture. "I just think they look pretty together," he said.

Straker shook his head. "Very weird," he commented.

The Playleader pocketed his photos. "What's your other reason?" he asked.

Straker gave a shifty look around him, leaned forward, and muttered, "Gotta pick somethin up down here. Riley sent me."

"I don't know him do I?"

"Sure you do," Straker said. "Young Denis's father."

"Ah yes," the Playleader said. "Him. Yes. He's got quite a lot of stuff back there now. Radios. Televisions. Couple of cameras."

"I just want a little brown paper parcel. You got that?"

"That's right," the Playleader nodded. "Wrapped in string. No address. I'll get it."

"I'll wait," Straker said, putting out a restraining hand. "I'll wait till I go." He lit another cigarette, eyeing the Playleader in an amused sort of way. "Funny you being tied in with Artie Riley," he said.

"Tell me about him," the Playleader said. "He's on the fiddle, isn't he?"

Straker laughed. "Bit more than a fiddle," he said. "Very big Artie is. Big connections."

"Well," the Playleader said doubtingly, "there can't be much in the odd TV set, can there?"

Straker was silent.

"You've known him a long time, have you?" the Playleader enquired.

"Artie? Oh yes. Ages. He's a little bit older than me, about Frank's age, see. But we was all mates back then. He was one of the boys, you know, with Frank and Terry and that. A very cool cat in his day. He used to live in the same street as me and Frank— where the estate is now—and we'd have our bikes out there, one, two, three in a row outside our houses. He was a big tearaway, Artie. Now . . . he just sits back and lets the money roll in. Lets others do the work for him. Good luck to him!"

"It's funny," said the Playleader reflectively. "He really seems much older than Frank and you. Like another generation."

"Ah, it's the beat keeps you young," Straker chuckled. Then grew serious. "That's how Frank sees it. He really does. He can't

stand the way Riley turned out. Despises him for it. You heard
all that stuff down at Rube's?" The Playleader nodded. "See," said
Straker, "for us lot then there were only so many ways to get by,
you know, the way things were. Now Artie's done it by makin
money. It's taken him a long time. It's bin hard. But he's ready
now to really clean up. Frank and me done it a different way wiv
the music and the gear and a laugh wiv the boys. It's bin all right.
We had good times. But now . . ." He shook his head. "I reckon it's
gettin a bit late in the day. But Frank won't see it. He's falling apart
and he won't see it. Artie wants to help him out, set 'im up, and he
won't let 'im."

"Why not?" asked the Playleader.

Straker flipped his fag end at the fence. "'Cause our good little
Frankie won't face up to it that you gotta take a coupla risks if you
want to make it like Artie's makin it."

The Playleader thought of the rather unexciting collection of
consumer durables in the rear of the hut. It all seemed rather a lot
of fuss about nothing very much. "But you're going in for good
with Riley?" he asked.

"Looks like it."

They sat in silence for a while. Gloria's friend brought out to
them some pink lemonade she'd been making.

"Frank says he's sorry, by the way," Straker said suddenly.
"About what happened down at Rube's. He's been thinkin it over.
He'd like to see you again. Say sorry and that."

"I couldn't go down to that café again, Straker."

"No, no. Frank don't want that neither."

"He's welcome to come up here," the Playleader said gra-
ciously. "I bear no grudges."

Straker nodded. "I'll tell 'im," he said. "Perhaps he'll come up."

They gazed sleepily around the Playground. Away on the other
side of the hill, from Harmon's little shanty where a small portable record player was installed, the insistent beat of reggae music
drifted faintly down to the concrete hut. One of those periods
of full and heavy calm had descended on the Playground. Some
boys were lazily painting the lower rungs of the climbing frame.
There was hardly any other movement. Even the tarzan rope went

unused, hanging still from the high tree in the warm dense late-afternoon air.

Straker sighed and stretched and settled back in his chair, reaching out a hand for his mug of pink lemonade. "Christ!" he breathed. "Aint this the life!"

When Straker had gone, the Playleader, his memory prompted by the reggae sounds, went up to Harmon's place to pay over the weekly seven quid. Harmon was inside with Facey, who was fast asleep on the little hut's earth floor, and with a pretty black girl with a striking afro, who was known mainly in the Playground as "Harmon's tart". Her name, the Playleader was pretty sure, was Donna. She sat, with a stack of 45s on her lap, over by the record player.

When Harmon put away the protection money, he revealed a wallet crammed full with banknotes. The Playleader regarded them with surprise, for it was not long since Harmon had regularly been bumming cigarettes off him. Harmon, seeing his wonder, laughed happily at him.

"This is a big fuckin summer, man," he said. "There's *so* much fuckin bread about."

The Playleader asked curiously, "Is Denis making money too?"

Harmon grimaced. "That fuckin Denis," he said. "He's just a teef."

"A what?"

"A teef, man," Harmon spoke impatiently. "He steals tings. Like his old man."

"Don't you."

"I sell em, man," said Harmon proudly. "I'm no teef."

"What do you sell?"

Harmon smiled. Then he said, "I saw you down there wit that Straker just now."

"Oh you know Straker?" asked the Playleader, surprised.

"I seen him around," Harmon said. "He's a mate of old man Riley right?"

"That's right," said the Playleader.

"He wants to watch out," the girl Donna said suddenly. "Dirty sod. He had a go at my friend's little brother."

"Oh . . ." the Playleader faltered. "I don't think he means any harm."

"Dirty sod," the girl repeated. "He wants to watch out."

"He wants to watch out anyway," Harmon said quietly. "Him an that fuckin Riley. They're really gonna get *fucked.*" He caught the Playleader gazing at him in bewilderment. He spread his hands and smiled, a fifteen-year-old again. "Well," he said, "'ats what I hear around. I wouldn't know. . . ." He studied the Playleader's puzzled face. "Ah, come on, man," he said cheerfully. "It's a hot day, right?" He prodded Facey awake with his toe. "Get up, you blood clout!" he yelled, kicking at Facey and clapping the Play-leader on the back simultaneously. "An go get some wine for my man here!"

6

As the day approached on which Portia Epstein was to visit the Playground, the Playleader found himself looking forward to their meeting more and more pleasurably. Surprised, he discovered that once again—after many months of drought—the thought of another woman was intriguing him. It was not really a sexual thing—although, God knew, it would have provided a respite from Alice who now unvaryingly treated him with no more than a distant civility, in and out of bed. Simply he remembered the strange mixture Portia had displayed—the clever astringency of her personality and the nonsense of her writing—with amusement and interest.

Alice behaved particularly nastily on the morning Portia was due. The Playleader had dressed himself, not in his usual Play-ground outfit of work-shirt and levis, but in a fairly stylish Kens-ington Market costume. He looked quite glorious in the mirror, he thought. But Alice was unmoved.

"You're such a pseud," she snapped. "You've got all the wrong ideas."

"Nobody asked you," he said coolly, tying up his silk necker-chief.

"You really think you're going to impress her, don't you?" Alice sneered, her brief-case in her hand. "You're so unsubtle."

"Fuck off, Alice," he said, not moving from the mirror. She went out, slamming the door on a final, loud *"Pathetic!"* The Playleader fitted on his glossy, high, square-toed leather boots and went to spoon out two helpings of instant coffee against Portia's arrival.

But when she arrived, half-an-hour later, she didn't want to stay for coffee or orange-juice or any other thing he offered her. Instead she hustled him off into the Mini and, five minutes after her arrival at his door, they were bowling down the road towards the south side of the river.

"How long does it take to get there," she asked.

"Fifteen to twenty minutes," he told her.

"Time enough," she muttered mysteriously.

He was much aware of her presence next to him. From time to time he peeped across at her. She was dressed in the same black outfit as before with the addition now of a cartridge belt around her waist. In the clear morning light he saw that she was older than he had thought before. Definitely in her late late thirties. Really ripe. He thought over possible conversation-openers.

"Speak into this," she told him abruptly. Her fist was held out beneath his chin. Focusing upon it, he saw that she was holding a tiny microphone to his mouth. Following with his eyes the narrow lead that dropped from her hand, he discovered upon her lap a tiny cassette tape recorder. "Speak into this," she said again. "I want to test the sound-level."

"What shall I say?"

"Anything. But in a normal voice." He looked ahead of him, to the right, and then across to her, searching for inspiration. He noticed the vivid flash of red upon her sleeve.

"Why do you wear that Danish flag?" he asked, concentrating on producing a normal voice for her.

She stopped the tape, re-wound it, then played it back. His voice sounded shy and apprehensive: "Why do you wear that Danish flag?" She stopped it again, looked up, and solemnly told him, "For a Dane." Then she started the tape recorder once more and spoke to the microphone.

"All right. OK. Now this playleading. Tell me about it." She held out the microphone to him.

"Well . . . what?"

She stopped the tape recorder with a frown. "Oy vay," she sighed. "Come on! I have to get inside your head if this is to work."

"I'm sorry," he said contritely. "I'll try."

"I'll ask you some more direct questions," she said more patiently. "Perhaps that'll jog you." She clicked the button on the tape recorder. "Now . . . how did you get into this play thing?" The microphone popped up in front of his face.

"I answered an ad in the paper," he told her truthfully. He glanced timidly across to find her raising her eyes to the car roof.

"But what got you *into* it?" she said to the microphone. "What *attracted* you? You like children, for instance?"

"Oh . . . I don't know. Sometimes. You know."

"Have you always worked with kids? Teaching and so on?"

"Oh no. No, this is the first time."

"What were you before?"

"Um . . . I worked in a factory last winter. Making Easter eggs."

"But what did you do before that?"

". . . I drove a van for a month."

"But before that. I mean what are you *really*? What did you *start* as?"

"Well . . . I *started*, I suppose, as an architect, sort of."

"How do you mean 'sort of'?"

"I don't mean 'sort of' really. I guess I *was* an architect. . . . But that's all over now."

"Why is it?"

"Just is."

"Did your buildings fall down?"

"I never put any up. You see, I wasn't long out of college when I quit."

"Well, why did you?"

"Don't know."

"Were you any good at it?"

He was silent, concentrating on getting round a slow lorry.

"Yes, I was," he said at last.

"Really?"

He laughed. "I actually was. My designs won medals, you know. And I got into a top firm when I graduated . . . I was a star, I really was." He shook his head.

"But then you just quit?"

"That's right."

"Still, why?"

He shook his head. "I don't know. I had to."

She frowned. "Aren't you curious why?"

"I don't think about it."

"Were you ill?"

". . . Tired."

"Were you into dope?"

"No . . . not that way."

"I can't believe you're so careless about it. I mean . . . your whole life changing like that."

It was his turn to frown. "Come on," she said sharply. "Tell!"

"It wasn't such a big thing. I just didn't want to do it any more. It palled on me. I got *tired*."

They were silent. Then she asked, "Do you miss it?"

"I miss . . . some things about it."

"Do you regret quitting?"

He didn't answer her.

She lit a Salem cigarette with one hand, still holding the microphone with the other. Looking down at her lap she said softly, "How did Alice feel about it?"

The Playleader smiled. "Oh, she was great," he said. "No reproaches. She just said she only wanted me to, you know, do what I want to do."

"And what's that?"

"I haven't found it," he said shortly.

"And she reckons you should have by now?"

He was silent. Then he burst out, "I don't know what the fuck's on her mind these days."

"You think she's not happy?" Portia said slowly.

"What do you think?"

"I think it's obvious," she said briefly. She looked out of her window. They were passing the tall towers of the Herbert Morrison Buildings. She told him, "Alice is a bright girl. And a good-looking one. She's making friends just now with some important people. Who like her and could help her along. She has a chance to go places. Maybe sometimes she feels you hold her back."

The Playleader was angry. "Since I never see her hardly," he said coldly. "I don't know how that could be."

"Oh you manage it," said Portia, equally coldly. "Husbands *do*, just by existing. You live in the back of her mind, don't you? Just supplying that little check here and there, and keeping her on your level. Don't you? And she has to come home nights of course, doesn't she? Which isn't too cool for an ambitious girl. Is it?"

"She didn't even do that when she visited *you*," he said, unearthing a grudge that he hadn't really realised existed.

"Yes," she snapped, clicking off the tape recorder, "and she made a lot of progress that night too."

He parked the car just outside the park's gates, and they walked inside and along the path that led to the Playground. It was a favourite time of his. Early morning, when the park smelled fresh and young, awakening after the night and empty of people.

As they walked beside the wire fence towards the Playground gates, she said to him, with a touch of embarrassment in her voice, "Listen, forget it. I'm sorry. It came out all wrong."

He was gazing over the fence at his Playground. She touched his arm, awarded him a rare smile. "I mean, it's a shame," she said. "You're quite likeable after all."

As usual the first job of the day was to bring the ropes round into the Playground and get them up on the trees. And as usual the Playleader started by hurting himself wriggling along the hump-backed branch of the low tree near the hut. Portia, standing below, called out in sympathy, "Hey, let me help!"

He shook his head, both to say no and to clear the pain. "It's tricky," he said.

"Shit!" she cried, "I can still get up trees."

So he let her take on a couple of the smaller trees, and since she was so competent at the task—leaping confidently at the lower branches, hauling herself athletically to the top—he let her do the tarzan rope tree as well. For the first time he hadn't to start the day with his stomach churning from the effort and panic of climbing that monstrous tall growth. A blessed relief.

A few early arrivals gathered under the tree to watch her at work, high above them, trim and efficient in her black uniform. "What's up there?" they asked, wondering.

"A bird, a plane—my lady assistant," the Playleader told them.

After Portia had returned to earth, the setting-up of a new contraption that he had devised the week before occupied them for some time. It centred around two rubber tyres which hung from short ropes attached to a much longer rope which was suspended between two trees thirty feet apart. The apparatus had to be hung just right, at just the proper distance from the ground and with the correct degree of tautness in the long rope. When it was up, two kids at a time could ride the tyres while somebody else—usually the Playleader until his hands developed painful blisters—pulled them to and fro by means of yet another rope tied to the long cross-rope and trailing to the ground. Anyway, until it was up in all its splendour, it was a jumble of tyres and ropes and knots and kids shouting "I'm first!" and "Pull me mister!"

When it was in place and two children—victors in a series of bloody combats (one of them, surprisingly, was Blaise in a torn shirt and with snot hanging from his nose)—had won the right to board the tyres first, the Playleader started the apparatus moving until his sore hands forced him to quit. Then Portia took over, pulling on the rope with mighty tugs, sending the children in wide, high arcs so that they screamed out in fright and pleasure. The Playleader sat on the grass and studied the woman, amused at the thoughtful concentration on her dark face as she heaved and strained at her task.

After ten minutes she threw the rope aside (to howls of protest from the occupants of the tyres) and turned laughing to face the Playleader.

"Wow! That's exercise!" she cried, pulling off her combat

jacket. Charmed by the sight of her nice full breasts under the black T-shirt, he held out his hand for her to pull him to his feet. Which, after a moment's hesitation, she did. They wandered towards the hut. They stopped beside the tarzan rope tree. Already a long queue had formed, and the rope was snaking back and forth under the tree carrying each time a child clutching on to it tight with hands and arms and legs.

As they watched, a boy sprang from one of the platforms onto the back of another boy who was already on the rope. The two rode together across to the other end of the arc and back again to the platform. And as they neared it, another boy hurled himself on top of them. Now all three swung together.

"Shit, that looks dangerous," marvelled Portia.

"That's boarding," the Playleader told her. "They're very good at it."

"I'd like a go on that rope," she said, looking up at the high bough from which it hung. "It looks fun."

"Well, have a go then," he said.

She looked at the boarding platform. "There's a huge long line for it," she said, pointing.

"So we'll barge in," he said.

"That's not fair," she protested.

"But we're bigger," he said, "and besides it's my Playground."

So, after a bitter little battle with the waiting queue of children, Portia was ensconced upon the rope, her legs on either side of the big knot on its end. The Playleader encouraged her from below.

"I don't know about this knot," she cried, fluttering.

"Just sit back on it and hang on tight!"

"But if I sit tight," she shouted, "what do I push myself off with? I mean, I got no way to propel myself like this."

"Somebody push her off," ordered the Playleader.

Eager hands shoved Portia in the small of her back. With an excited whoop, she was off the platform and travelling fast towards the other side.

"Hey, this is *fun!*" she shrieked, flashing past the Playleader. He was enchanted to see upon her face, always so reserved and ironic, the most enormous grin. Then as he watched, her expression changed once more, now to comic dismay as, on her re-approach to the platform, she saw a youth preparing to board her.

"No, you little bastard, you don't!" she yelled, kicking out. But in vain. The boy swooped upon her and, on the bucking, swinging rope they clung together for dear life, arcing through the air three, four and five times until the rope slowed, the boy jumped off, and at last Portia could rest her feet, tentatively, upon solid ground.

"Oh!" she cried breathlessly, "Oh wow!"

They continued on their way towards the hut, she still marvelling over her adventure. "I couldn't believe that little kid!" she exclaimed, laughing. "Why he was grabbing at my tits all the way, the little prick! I mean two handfuls full. I couldn't believe it!"

"But you liked it?" the Playleader asked, settling her into one of the chairs that Gloria's friend had once again thoughtfully brought out into the pleasant morning sunshine. "The rope, I mean."

"Oh fantastic!" she said. "Wild ride. It was really great." She touched his arm. "Thank you."

Then Gloria's friend herself appeared before them, picking up Portia's gesture with inquisitive eyes. "I've sent Piers off to get some coffee," she announced. "He'll be back soon."

Portia was fascinated. "Hello charmer," she said to the little girl, leaning forward and smiling.

"Who's she?" Gloria's friend asked the Playleader. "Alice?"

"No," the Playleader assured her, "A friend."

The child stagily lowered her voice. "That's good," she murmured spitefully. "She's a bit old for you, isn't she?"

"Sorry about that," the Playleader told Portia, when Gloria's friend had gone inside the hut. "I guess it's true. You women just can't get along."

Portia smiled grimly. "Oh we *can*," she told him, "if we *try*."

They smoked Salems and gazed comfortably at the now-teeming Playground. Piers arrived with two mugs of coffee from the café. The little boy was fascinated by the military aspects of Portia's costume. He sat on the ground in front of them, fingering the sergeant's stripes on the sleeve of her combat jacket.

"I'm going to be a soldier when I'm old," he told them.

"What for?" Portia asked, a mite chidingly.

"To kill people," the child said with relish.

A little later Harmon and Denis came into the Playground together, talking intensely. But when they noticed Portia and the Playleader they smiled, ambled over and, shoving Piers out of the way, squatted on their haunches before the chairs.

"This your old lady?" Denis enquired.

"I'm a friend! I'm a friend!" Portia said laughing.

"She's from America," the Playleader told them.

"Oh yeah?" Denis said politely.

Harmon said, "I got relatives there, you know. Brownsville. You know that place?" Portia didn't. "Well, I got relatives there," Harmon repeated firmly.

Conversation languished. Denis kept looking worriedly at Harmon who kept his eyes moodily downcast. The Playleader watched them both, puzzled. Suddenly Harmon reached out a long brown arm and touched the Playleader with a forefinger on his chest. "Hey, you tell this fucker here to watch out for himself." He stood up. "Maybe he'll listen to you." He walked away.

"What was all that about?" the Playleader asked, astonished.

Denis was frowning at the dust. "Bovver," he said tersely, at last. "There's a bit of trouble round here." He looked up at the Playleader's bewildered face and smiled reluctantly. "You don't have a clue, do you, mate?" he said kindly. And he stood up too. "Pleased to have met you," he nodded politely at Portia, and went off towards his shanty.

The Playleader answered her unspoken question. "I don't *know*," he said. "Something's up. *I* don't know what."

"They treat you as if *you* were the kid," she marvelled.

"Oh well," he told her with a certain pride, "they've grown up fast down here this summer."

For a while they drowsed together in the sun. Then some kids came and took the Playleader away to admire the new hut they had put up at the back of the hill. Portia in the meantime got out her reporter's note-book and made some entries, checking around the Playground with careful eyes.

While the Playleader was away back of the hill, the Park-keeper paid one of his rare visits to the Playground and, finding an unoccupied chair and a fairly captive audience, planted himself firmly down beside Portia. When the Playleader returned the old man was gassing away in his usual vein, and the woman was sweating lightly with the effort of hearing him out. The Playleader brought out another chair and placed it on the Park-keeper's other side.

"Here, he'll tell you," the old man told Portia, acknowledging the Playleader's arrival with a wave of his arm. "Ever since he's been here his life's been ruddy hell. Sodding blacks have walked all over him. Haven't they, mate? Haven't they? You tell her then."

"Oh come on!" the Playleader urged, dismayed at the look of strain in Portia's eyes. "You exaggerate."

"What did I say?" the Park-keeper complacently asked Portia. "The trouble is, of course," he nattered on, "the *fundamental* error is the treating your races the same. I mean," he waved his hands again to include the whole scene before them, "you and me and your normal white person, what do we see when we look around? We see a playground, right? But your average blackie on the contrary, looking at all them trees and dangling ropes and all, he sees something *fundamentally* different." He glanced to either side. Portia and the Playleader were staring uncomfortably ahead. "What do they see?" the Park-keeper demanded. Then triumphantly answered his question: "They see a sodding great jungle. Home sweet home!" he cackled. "Right? And they go sodding *mad*! Am I right?" He leaned over and tapped the Playleader on his knee. "That's the root of your troubles son. That's your root."

The Playleader could endure no more. "You're an ignorant, stupid, bigoted, reactionary old fool!" he burst out.

"Right on!" cried Portia excitedly from the Park-keeper's far side.

There was a moment's silence. Then the Park-keeper's complaining whine resumed. "That's as maybe. I'm not prepared to say you haven't got a point there. But you young blokes, you're too young to know what this country was like without the blackies. Smashing place it was. Apart from a few Yids and Irish you knew what everybody was thinking. Now I read this paper, see— I'll bring you a copy—it's called *British Action*. Now there are facts in there about your blacks in Britain you wouldn't believe. For instance, did you know . . ." And the old man drivelled on and on, while first Portia and then the Playleader fell gratefully into deep and peaceful slumbers.

7

THE PLAYLEADER WAS woken by a heavy hand upon his shoulder. He looked up startled to see big Frank dropping heavily into the now-vacant chair between himself and Portia, who still slept on, her mouth ungracefully but rather affectingly wide-open.

"Who's the bint?" Frank asked. "The wife?"

The Playleader said no. "Straker told me you might be coming up," he added. "And listen . . . there's no need to apologise, Frank, about what happened down at Rube's. I understand perfectly."

"I aint plannin to apologise," Frank said shortly. "I was perfectly in me rights bungin you out. You dint get hurt did yer? So what are you on about?"

"*I'm* not on about anything, Frank," the Playleader said earnestly. "I wish the whole thing was over and forgotten. It's just that Straker . . ." His voice tailed off. Frank was rolling a cigarette from a tin of A1 tobacco on his lap. He licked the gummed strip and looked sidelong at the Playleader.

"It's Straker I'm up here about," he said.

The Playleader was puzzled. "What about Straker?"

Frank was silent. Then snapped, "Stoopid little bugger!" He brooded for a while, then said in a calmer voice, "He's in trouble, see?"

"What sort of trouble?" the Playleader enquired.

"You know Art Riley," Frank stated.

"Yes," said the Playleader, "I've met him."

"I heard you done some business wiv 'im."

"Oh," the Playleader shrugged. "Look, I just let him keep some things in here."

"That's what I heard," Frank said gloomily. "You wanna be careful."

"Oh Christ!" the Playleader snorted. "Go and look if you want.

He's got, I think, one TV set in there, which I don't even think is new, and an electric lawn mower. Now what's there to get excited about in that? Go on, have a look at them."

"All right, I believe you," said Frank. He sighed gustily. "That's the fuckin trouble. I can't see what Artie's up to."

Portia then woke up, frowning and blinking in the now-strong sunlight.

"Tell 'er to take a walk," Frank ordered the Playleader impatiently.

"Screw you!" she cried, outraged.

The Playleader urged Frank to join him on a stroll round the Playground and, after exchanging a couple of nasty glances with Portia, the big man heaved himself up and followed the Playleader.

"Now, what trouble is Straker in?" the Playleader asked again.

"All I know is that there's bad feeling about whatever Art Riley's up to and that Straker's in wiv 'im in a big way. It's somethin else than the usual nickin Art does. Somethin bigger. I know Straker's bin down here runnin errands. I thought you might have some idea about it."

The Playleader shook his head. "Really I can't help you," he said.

Frank swore. The Playleader said awkwardly, "You're really worried about him?"

"Course I am," Frank said angrily. "'Stoopid little git!" He strode across the grass frowning. The Playleader hurried to keep up. "It's not worth it, mate," Frank told him despairingly. "I seen it happen to Art. He don't dare go out these days wivout a coupla boys. He's too fuckin scared to. You ever see 'im 'appy? Now fuckin stoopid Straker wants to go the same way. Too fuckin greedy for 'is own good."

They arrived at the Playground gate. "If I see him, do you want me to ask him to contact you?" asked the Playleader.

"Yeah," Frank said grimly. "Tell 'im to get smart an all too . . . Yeah," he said again. "Tell 'im to get in touch."

Portia remarked when the Playleader sat down beside her again, "You get some really weird people visiting you here, don't you though?"

Towards evening, Portia, who had been scribbling for a half-hour concentratedly, passed her note-book across to him. "This is for the paper," she said.

He took a deep breath and read:

Imagine me in an island in a city in a borough in a park imagine a green haven of trees and kids and ropes and kids and sun and kids and little huts containing kids and over us all imagine presiding a jolly gentle giant . . .

"You're no fan of mine," she smiled at his expression.

"Well . . . Let me read it all." He did so. Then said, "It's very flattering."

"It's how it strikes me."

"This jolly gentle giant . . . is that God or me?"

"You. Dummy!"

"You can't really say I'm a *giant*."

"Well . . . you're quite tall."

"You like this Playground though?" he asked.

"Didn't I write that?"

"But you do?"

"Yes," she said, "you're doing nice things here."

"I'm doing nothing hardly here."

"Well . . . that's nice too."

He proposed a last wander before they took the ropes down—up the hill, round by the clump of plane trees, along the fence.

She said, "You seem happy here too."

"Oh, but it's not much, is it?" he said. "It's like Alice says: 'Messing around with kids.'"

"So what, if you like it? What does it matter?"

"It matters. Because she *doesn't* like it."

Portia was silent.

"It's understandable," the Playleader said. He bent to pick up a stump of wood which had a nail protruding dangerously from it. "Like you said, she's ambitious. She wants to live a certain way, with certain people. She's ambitious for herself, ambitious for me. I don't blame her."

Still Portia was silent.

"If I want her," declared the Playleader, "I have to accept that. I know we're drifting apart because she despises what I do, what I've become."

"You're sure that's the reason," the woman asked.

"What else?" She didn't answer. "Anyway," he went on, "that's all I can think of."

"So what will you do?"

"Well," he said slowly, "I had an offer of a job. It's not very . . . Alice would like it better. Better than the factory anyway, better than this place." He told her about the lectureship Tenby had put up to him. "I turned it down then. But the way Alice and me have been going, I have to do something drastic. Perhaps she'll see it as a step in her direction at least."

"Well," his companion said, "it seems sad. Especially if the problem is something else."

"But what could it be. Can you think of anything else?"

But all she said was, "Well, take care. Look out for yourself."

At the end of the day, when the ropes had been stored away in the hut and the gates locked for the night, the Playleader suggested a drink in a pub. Portia said no. He offered her a lift home. She accepted one to the nearest tube. In the car, moistening his lips nervously, he said, "I've liked today."

She agreed it had been nice. Warming to his task, he said, "It'd be nice to see you again, perhaps."

Looking up, surprised, she said, "I expect I'll see you around."

"But why don't we *organise* a meeting," he urged. "Maybe I could come round to see you at your place." She was silent. He pressed on. "I could do it easily. Alice is away all the time."

Now she said loudly, in an astonished voice, "Could you *possibly* be propositioning *me*?"

Flustered, he said, "Well . . . yes. Baldly. That's so."

She laughed gleefully. "Oh, too much!" she cried. She looked across at him, shaking her head. "You're amazing. This hasn't happened to me in . . . wow! years!"

"It was just an idea," he muttered.

"I can't believe you don't . . . well . . ." She chuckled to herself. "And I believed you were so tied up with sweet Alice too."

"Oh I *am*," he said firmly, nodding his head. "We have an arrangement though of course. *She* won't mind. As long as we're discreet."

"Well," Portia said, "that's nice. But *I'd* mind. Quite a lot."

"OK," he shrugged. "I'm sorry I don't appeal."

"Oh it's not *you*," she said. Then, surprisingly, giggled. "It's your *type*."

And from then until the tube station they never said a word to one another, although, irritating for him, Portia from time to time let loose a loud and merry chuckle.

8

THE PLAYLEADER HAD been quite serious when he had talked to Portia about accepting the lecturing job. He fully intended to contact Tenby and tell him of his decision. But several days went by and he did not do it. Often, waking up in the morning—Alice a reproachful lump on the other side of the bed—he told himself "I'll ring him today no matter what." But whenever he got near a phone, a terrifying vision of obscure and ignominious drudgery oppressed him so deeply that his nerve failed him every time.

Still, he was not sorry—though naturally surprised—to discover on his return from the Playground one evening, Tenby himself a guest in his flat.

When the Playleader came in, Tenby was on his knees on the living room carpet surrounded by photographs, an untidy pile of typescript, and another new friend, Jonathan Ames. The latter smiled benevolently at the Playleader's entrance. "I've been hoping we wouldn't miss you," he called out.

Alice, eyeing her husband moodily, informed him, "I'm just going out for some booze. You don't want any."

The Playleader was amused and braced at the look of surprise on Tenby's face. "No," he told Alice jauntily, "I don't care for that, as you know. But," he intercepted the joint that was passing between Jonathan and Tenby, "I'm partial to this."

When Alice had gone, Tenby went into the bedroom where the Playleader was changing out of his grubby Playground outfit.

"Christ, it's a small world," Tenby said. He looked flustered. "I had no idea there was any connection, you know, between Alice and you. . . . I can't remember. Did I ever say anything? Er—she's a great girl, you know. Congratulations."

The Playleader thanked him; then, with a deep breath, offered to take the lecturing job. Tenby was ecstatic. The Playleader asked him not to tell Alice. "It's a surprise for her," he said.

Tenby was touched. "Not a word," he promised.

An anguished howl from Jonathan brought them back into the living room. He was sitting cross-legged on the carpet, shifting through the photos and typescript. "It just doesn't make it, man," he said to Tenby sorrowfully.

The Playleader stooped to pick up some photographs. They were of children, all of them pretty, the boys mostly in long hair and turtle-neck sweaters. Some were of groups of children. In these there was almost always one—no more—black child, invariably in the front row, but a little off-centre. One of the groups had a Chinese child, but she had only made it to far left, second row.

"What's the problem?" asked the Playleader.

"It's this damn book we're doing," Jonathan sighed, "it's just not fat enough."

"What's it about?" the Playleader asked, replacing the photographs.

"You remember," Tenby said. "I mentioned it to you. The kids and TV thing. What's the point of it, Jonathan?"

"Well, what we say is," Jonathan said, checking the top page of the manuscript, "that 'the institutionalisation of a young individual's role-expectations in the pseudo-cathartic violence of the average children's television programme is bound ultimately to lead to a malfunction of his essential need-dispositional mechanisms—'"

"Etcetera, blah, blah," Tenby cut in. "Well, it's a point of view," he argued, "and we put it over fairly well."

"But at no great length," said Jonathan moodily. "Tenby, we just don't have enough here."

"Come and think about it with us," Tenby told the Playleader, settling himself down on the carpet. The Playleader sat down with him. Tenby handed him a thin sheaf of typescript.

"Now," he said, "we got about—what, Jonathan?—fifteen thousand words in there?"

"No more than that. I doubt if it's that high."

"Well," Tenby carried on, weighing the manuscript in his hands, "that's what we got. And even in large type it doesn't make a book."

"Write some more?" suggested the Playleader.

The other two groaned. "God, man!" Tenby cried, "I've already spent two fucking days over a typewriter. Enough already. It doesn't come that easy, you know."

"Well . . ." pondered the Playleader, "can't you cram it full of pictures?"

Jonathan shook his head. "Alice says no more than eight. She says it'll be too expensive otherwise. The publishers couldn't afford it."

"Profit-mongers!" rasped Tenby bitterly.

The Playleader shrugged. "It'll have to be a very slim volume then," he told them. "What else can you do?"

Tenby this time shook his head. "Might as well not do it then. No use telling people that you've done a book, then coming up with a nasty little dwarf of a thing. Especially with *two* authors, I mean . . . No," he said firmly, "it has to be one inch thick at least."

The Playleader shrugged again. Tenby took a thoughtful drag on the now rather damp and sticky joint. "I have some hopes," he announced, "of the end-papers."

Jonathan stirred. "How do you mean?"

"Well," said Tenby, "you know. We'll have the title on . . . oh, at least three different pages up front and then we'll have a dedication page—a snatch of verse and a mention of my mother. Well, in fact, since there are two of us we could arguably have *two* dedications on *two* pages. No? And then there'll be your Acknowledgements. The people who helped us in the making of this book."

"Who were they?" Jonathan asked curiously.

Tenby waved his hands. "Everybody. Why not? Alice, for instance, and"—he nodded at the Playleader—"him. And we can have everybody who's been a sort of spiritual aid, of course. All those sporty people. Duke of Edinburgh, Chay Blythe, all that crowd. . . . We'll squeeze three pages out of that lot. At least."

"What else?" asked Jonathan.

"Appendices in the back," Tenby rattled on. "We'll stick in all the quotes from other books we didn't get into the text."

"Christ, there aren't many of them," Jonathan said worriedly. "I have a conscience about them already. I think we overdid it."

Tenby ignored him. "Bibliography," he cried. "Three more pages out of that."

"Index?" the Playleader suggested.

Tenby pounded him on the back. "Ten pages!" he cried excitedly. "Easily."

"Jesus, who'll do an index for us? It'll cost money."

"I can find a hack'll do it for two guineas," Tenby promised. "*And* we'll have cross-references and everything."

"Well," said the Playleader, "now you have your book." But Tenby, who was doing sums on his fingers, said dejectedly, "No. Not quite. Bugger it!"

Tenby sat and thought. Jonathan, honest face ablush, whispered to the Playleader. "Me, I deplore this kind of thing. But Tenby . . . !" Tenby waved him quiet.

The Playleader's face brightened. "An introduction," he offered. "Somebody could write you an introduction."

Tenby gave a whoop. "Beautiful!" he shouted.

"An introduction." Jonathan thought it over. "That sounds legitimate. Very nice."

"Perfect," Tenby said, "a thousand words in big type and we're home and dry."

"But who'll do it for you?" the Playleader enquired.

Tenby said, "I've already thought of that. You will."

"Me!"

"Why him?" asked Jonathan. "Oh. You mean as a playleader?"

"Better still," beamed Tenby, "as a Lecturer in Recreational Science."

He briefed Jonathan on the Playleader's academic prospects. Jonathan commiserated with the Playleader. "Shitty for you," he told him, "but good for our book, I must say."

"Oh, but I can't write," the Playleader protested. "I really can't. Besides, I don't know what the book's about."

"Read it," Tenby recommended.

"Come on," Jonathan reproved him, "that's hardly fair."

They sat in sad silence.

"I would if I could," the Playleader ventured. Nobody responded.

Suddenly Tenby stood up. "Hell, *I'll* do it," he said. "Can we use your name at least?" he asked the Playleader.

"Of course. Do."

"Then I'll do it. Be best anyway, I guess. You wouldn't know what tack to take." Tenby picked up a couple of sheets of blank paper and a pencil and retired to the bedroom. Jonathan and the Playleader sat in nervous silence until Jonathan, with an embarrassed half-grin, said, "This is awful isn't it? So cheap. I don't know how I got roped into it. He's so . . . *corrupt*, isn't he?" Jonathan shuddered. "But one *has* to get ahead."

"Of course," agreed the Playleader.

After ten minutes Tenby, sweating profusely, reappeared, clutching his two now-scribbled pages. "Listen," he said, planting himself in the middle of the room and preparing to read. He glanced down at Jonathan. "Since I did the work I thought I'd give myself the major leg-up. OK? Right. Now then, it's supposed to be this"—nodding at the Playleader—"lecturer writing. . . . Here it goes." He coughed, focused on the page before him, and declaimed: "INTRODUCTION—I suppose there can be few individuals, even among those only marginally concerned with the problem of children's play, who can still be unaware of the life and labours of Neville Harrison—" Tenby broke off, looked down at Jonathan. "I'm sorry," he said, "I really have to do it. The old fart's been on my back very badly lately."

"Go on," Jonathan said. "It's OK."

"Almost single-handed," Tenby read, "Harrison has dragged the discipline, appropriately kicking and screaming, from out of the swaddling clothes of the nineteenth century into the blue jeans and T-shirts of the late twentieth. In the burgeoning field of Recreational Science, it may be truly said of Neville Harrison—and what a scandal it is that neither of our ancient universities has yet seen fit to grant him appropriate recognition—that he has made order where once was chaos and brought light where utter darkness reigned."

Tenby wiped his brow. "And that's all I'm doing for *him*," he said. "The rest is about us." He read on. "In this scintillating book, two of the most brilliant of Harrison's younger disciples examine some of the more fundamental questions which are confronting the academic study of children's play. Their joint efforts represent a major breakthrough—perhaps *the* major breakthrough—in the field over the past ten years—"

"Twenty?" suggested the Playleader, well into the spirit of the thing.

"Fuckit, I'll say fifty," Tenby muttered, correcting his manuscript. ". . . *the* major breakthrough in the field over the past *fifty* years. The two young authors are both leaders in their separate professions. Jonathan Ames"—Tenby bowed to his collaborator—"is a television producer, one of the seminal figures in the current renaissance in this quintessential medium of the 1970s—" He waved aside Jonathan's protests from the floor, and resumed: "P.A.S.W. Tenby, his co-author, who has written widely on many aspects of children's play (a short-list of titles appears in the rear of this volume), is, as Neville Harrison's valued, right-hand man in the Department of Recreation, centrally-placed in the drive to spread, upon the ground as it were, the new knowledge of ways and means in this field which is being developed by people like myself ('That's you,' Tenby told the Playleader) in the academies."

There were about five more minutes of this stuff. Tenby delved a little further into his own and Jonathan's backgrounds, touched on the (revolutionary) significance of their work, and ended with a recommendation that the book should be on the shelf of "everyone involved in Recreational Science; everyone who works in, writes about or even watches TV; everyone concerned about the future of children's play; everyone who welcomes the opportunity of watching two coruscating young intellects at work; and, finally, everyone who just—plain—likes—kids."

"I think that covers everything," Jonathan agreed.

Alice came back in time to hear the end. "What's that?" she asked.

"It's our Introduction," Jonathan told her.

"Who wrote it. It sounds terrible."

"Well," Tenby said annoyed, "I wrote it. But"—he caught the Playleader's warning glance—"but we're getting some lecturer or other to sign it."

Alice ruffled Jonathan's dark curly hair as she went past with the wine on her way to the kitchen. "Have you boys got enough pages together?" she asked.

"Just enough," Tenby called and trotted after her. The Playleader put some albums on the stereo while Jonathan carefully rolled another joint, balancing a record sleeve upon his knees to catch the precious flakes.

They had a pleasant evening. The smoke and the wine went round and round; even the Playleader had a sip. When they got tired of the records, Alice brought out her old guitar and they sang early Beatles numbers in bad harmony. It was all quite nostalgic. The Playleader remembered student life: classes at the Architectural Association and vile bed-sitters in Belsize Park. Looking at Alice, who for a wonder was looking at him with warm eyes as she banged away at the guitar, it seemed probable to him that she was thinking of the same things. For they had shared them together.

When the others, after sleepy sentimental goodbyes, had gone, husband and wife wandered smashed around the flat. She came over to him and nuzzled in the join of his neck and shoulder. He felt the hurt of the past weeks welling up inside. He held her wrists. "I don't want to be picked up and dropped again. It's not fair."

She said, teary-eyed, "No. I won't pick you up. I'm sorry about it."

He promised her then, "Things are going to change. You see. I got some plans."

She said, "All right. Perhaps they will. I don't know."

He told her, "I got it all worked out. You see."

Sad and drunk and stoned they went to bed and slept chastely together, in each others' arms for comfort.

AFTER ALL, THE actual business of getting the lectureship proved not to be as frightful as the Playleader had feared.

On the morning appointed for the interview, he had fished out from the back of a closet a sports jacket and had found a tie, wrinkled but still serviceable. Tenby, who had arranged, without pleasure and only because no-one else would do it, to take over the Playground for the day, met him at the railway terminus and, with motherly anxiety, dusted him down and tidied him up.

"Just look em straight in their eyes, old man," he advised.

In the train the Playleader watched the pleasant countryside speeding by and speculated on the prospect before him. The university he was destined for had a unique reputation. It was very new—a collection of stark white buildings set in chilly grandeur upon a bare heath in the rear of a town which had first developed as an eighteenth century spa. Yet, paradoxically, though new, it was tightly organised on the old Oxbridge college system, manners as well as structure. Everybody wore their gowns simply everywhere. Chapel was practically compulsory; dinner in hall definitely was, and there, of course, the dons all ate at high table.

The university had an intellectual fame beyond its years. Its senior members, almost to a man, were firmly in the van of what the Vice-Chancellor himself had recently described in the *Spectator* as a "new Conservatism, radical, divisive, and yes, if you like, bloody-minded even." It took an inordinate proportion of students from the Home Counties, very many of them from an oddly-limited collection of minor public schools. It had never had a student rebellion and it experienced no difficulty whatsoever in raising phenomenal sums from great corporations and trusts. It was all very impressive.

However, the interviewing committee which confronted the Playleader seemed none too formidable. Possibly, he thought, they were only a scratch lot, all that were available for it was still a few weeks before the beginning of term. Still, he liked them all, with reservations about one very old man who, disconcertingly, giggled at him from time to time in a high and silly tone. Nobody, it soon developed, had any idea what Recreational Science was all about and, since the Playleader couldn't really enlighten them, conversation soon languished.

After five minutes or so of utter silence, one of the junior members of the committee, a rather butch young man with a permanent sneer, growled "Hair's a bit long, isn't it?"

The Playleader assured him he'd get it cut off. At which the chairman of the committee knocked on the table, looked around him enquiringly, and said, "Well, that's about it. Unless anyone has any more . . . ?"

Nobody did. The chairman welcomed the Playleader onto the staff, assigned him to Lever College, of which he himself it turned out was Master, and led his new recruit off for sherry in his palatial rooms.

The Master had a pleasant light tan. He revealed that he was fresh back from a lecture tour in the United States over the summer.

"I believe I've brought back one nugget of truth from my little trip," he said. The Playleader leaned forward to hear it. "Always travel first-class," the Master advised, pouring a very little sherry in the Playleader's glass.

He was a fun old boy; the Playleader liked him. A little round butter-ball of a man in a tidy dark-blue suit and a blue and white spotted bow-tie. He was quite famous too, an historian with immense paper-back sales. His major work had been a three-volumed study of a sixteenth century statesman. There was an interesting story connected with his research. As a young scholar he had been entrusted with this statesman's papers—an incredibly rich and important source for all manner of topics within the period. After his own research was completed and many all-important items photographed or noted down in his neat little handwriting and placed in his files, the original papers were all destroyed in a mysterious fire. Providentially his files were unharmed. There had been quite a scandal at the time. But with his increasing reputation—and perhaps with changing times—the feeling grew that in fact the Master had pulled off a brilliant coup. From time to time he pulled a couple of shards from the goldmine in his files and used them to blast the fortunes of some rival historian who had unwarily strayed too close to his own preserves. Or else he used them simply to build up his own massive reputation a little higher still. Some of the very minor material he tossed to the hordes of wretched research students that flocked to his doors. He had sold job lots of it too to American universities and libraries during the lush 1960s. He was now a very rich man. As indeed these days was the university's present Vice-Chancellor who, unexpectedly to many, had appointed him to his Mastership.

"It's damned brutal hard work," he told the Playleader at the end of their meeting, "and I don't know why we do it. But it has its rewards, too. You'll see." And, cheered by his encouragement, the Playleader set off home in unexpectedly high spirits.

Oddly the feeling stayed with him even after he had paid a visit to the Playground on his way home from the railway terminus. The scene of devastation he found there was horrible of course. From the confused descriptions faltered out by a few frightened children he found lurking nearby, he was able to piece together the story of what had happened. Tenby had felt obliged to close the Playground ten minutes after its opening, for angry protests had greeted his decision not to put up any ropes that day. The protests had grown into scuffles, then escalated further into near riot proportions, a whirlpool of violence which had drawn into its stormy heart figures of ever-increasing authority and power— first the lady from the toddlers' One O'Clock Club next door, then assorted gardeners and park-keepers, finally a couple of brawny cops from the local station. Before the raging tumult was finally suppressed, an impressive amount of damage had been sustained: by the Playground—broken equipment, kicked-in shanties; and by the kids—bruises, bloody noses, and, in one sad case, the Play-leader's and Gloria's good friend, a quick trip to the hospital with a suspected broken leg. This last item especially depressed the Play-leader. But even so he could not help from time to time a warm, complacent glow spreading delightfully all over him as he contem-plated the day's disaster in the Playground. Evidently *here* at least he was utterly irreplaceable.

10

THE PLAYLEADER'S MOOD of cheery benevolence lasted a few more days. It was a good time generally. He was contentedly absorbed in the minutiae of resurrecting the Playground—debris clearing, equipment repairing, hospital visits—and at home life was now very much more stable and relaxed, with Alice out most evenings and, when at home, showing towards him a new tenderness which he found infinitely pleasing. Oddly, because they met so rarely in this time, the Playleader had no real opportunity to reveal to her the good news about his new job. He was waiting for just the right moment, and it was taking its own time in coming. Nevertheless, it was fun to look forward to the time when he *could* tell her, and he spent many hours happily anticipating her excitement and congratulations.

However. . . .

The day the roof fell in on the Playleader (cool and crisp with a hint of autumn in the air) he returned from the Playground at seven as usual to find Alice and Portia sitting side by side upon the sofa. He had not seen Portia since her disturbingly total rejection of him in the car, and he was a little shy to see her now. However, *she* seemed quite composed.

Alice, on the other hand, was clearly flustered, her fair face colouring at his entrance. She sat very stiffly on the sofa, leaning away from Portia who lounged far back in it, one booted leg across the other.

The Playleader sank into a chair opposite with a friendly nod to both of them.

"Dear," said Alice, "I want to tell you something."

"So do I," the Playleader said smiling, "but you go first."

"Dear," she began again. Then stopped and picked furiously at a loose thread on the hem of her skirt.

"Shit," said Portia. "Get on with it."

"It means something to *us*." Alice looked at her, annoyed. "You'd better leave us alone."

Portia went off huffily into the bedroom. The Playleader watched her go, then turned back apprehensively to his wife.

Alice said, "I'm going off with her, you know."

"Where?" he asked (hoping it was to the pictures).

"America."

"Oh . . . America. Um . . . for long?"

"I don't know."

He now was busy with a loose thread. "Are you leaving me or something?"

She agreed that she was. He leaned forward, appalled. "Look, things are going to change," he told her urgently. "I *told* you that. Things *have* changed. I've got this new job you'll like—"

"Yes. Portia said you were going for it," Alice said tenderly. "I'm so glad for you . . . if you think you'll like it."

"Doesn't it change everything?"

"No. Why should it?"

"Oh fuckit," he cried out in anguish. "*I* can take you away if you want to go. We'll go anywhere. Why must you go right now?"

"Because *she* has to go back now."

"So?"

She looked at him, seeming irritated. "You *know*," she said.

"I don't," he insisted. "Tell me."

She gazed at him. Then looked as if for help towards the room where Portia had gone. "I thought you knew," she sighed. "Well . . ." she started. And stopped again. Quickly she turned to pick up her handbag from the corner of the sofa. She fished inside and came up with a newspaper cutting. This she passed over to the Playleader. He glanced at it, then dropped it on the floor. It was another episode in Portia's "Seximental Journey".

"I don't want to read her crap just now," he said angrily.

"Read it," Alice said coldly, "if you want to know." Helpfully she added, "I'm 'A'."

He retrieved the clipping and began to read. Portia's piece this time was tumultuous with passion, a long, elaborate, bawdy description of a monster fuck between the author and her lover 'A' in which A's "pallid British thighs" and "rich ripe ruby tongue-deep gash" wove amazingly sensuous arabesques around every endless sentence. Even in his dismay the Playleader could not help experiencing himself a slight stirring down below.

But this went quite away when, at the bottom of the column, he read a terse dismissal of A's husband—"a creepy limey-nebbish who held my royal princess in dull straight thrall these eight past droughty summers." At that he looked up and to Portia, who had returned and was standing now behind Alice, one hand protectively on her lover's shoulders, he complained, "I thought I was the jolly gentle giant!"

"You're that too," she said gently. "The perspective changes, that's all."

He read on to the end, and then gazed miserably at the two women.

"We had arguments about whether or not you'd guessed," Alice told him. "Portia said you hadn't. But I said you *couldn't* be that dim."

"Well, I was." He handed back the newspaper clipping. "So it's been Portia all along? All those late nights."

"Yes," Alice said, touching the other woman's hand.

"Why didn't you tell me?"

"But that was part of our arrangement. Not to tell."

"Was it? I wasn't sure."

They stared at each other. There was something he felt he had to ask her, not knowing how much time was left. "Does it agree with you?"

"What?"

"With her."

"Um . . . yes."

"Better than . . . ?"

"Well . . . I just think it's *me* now. More natural."

"Who would have thought," he marvelled. ". . . What do you *do* exactly?"

"Oh for heaven's sake! It's almost entirely an emotional thing, you know."

"Yeah. I know . . . Still . . . go on, tell me."

"Well," she began. Then stopped, embarrassed. They tittered pruriently together.

Portia stamped her feet. "Jesus Christ!" she cried. "That's enough! You British! So *kinky!*"

Everything rushed forward. Cases appeared, new leather ones he had not seen before. Now Alice was putting on her coat. "I've left you practically everything," she told him. "It's all yours now."

He helped her into a sleeve. "Oh Alice!" he said tragically, his stomach lurching. "Aren't I ever going to see you again?"

"Let's get out of here," Portia urged. "This stuff . . . !"

"Of course you'll see me again," Alice told him, clutching his hands, her eyes searching his distraught face. "Almost certainly."

"When? . . . do you suppose?"

"Oh, we have long lives ahead of us," she said. "Sometime. Who knows? Perhaps next year we'll have another little pad together somewhere. You and me. Or me and you and Portia. Or whoever."

Portia was holding both cases. The front door was half-open. He moved towards his wife. They kissed. He implored her, "Alice! Eight years! You can't!"

She faltered. "You're right," she moaned, "I can't."

But Portia quickly put her foot down, and, as it turned out, Alice could.

II

IN FACT IT was not quite as simple as that. There followed a week of chaotic to-ing and fro-ing on everyone's part. Alice would appear on the Playleader's doorstep, tearful, desperate for a reconciliation. The next day she'd be gone again. One time Portia was round at his flat, demanding to know where the hell Alice was. He didn't know either and they spent a drunken, incoherent, not unfriendly evening together railing at Alice's fickle behaviour. Another time *he* was round at Portia's door, pleading through the letter-flap for a word from "My fucking wife, dammit!" He didn't get it. The whole messy period ended in a wild climax at the Cromwell Road air terminal which featured husband and wife weeping in each other's arms while Portia, bull-roaring in rage, belaboured Alice furiously about the head and shoulders with the TWA ticket folders.

On the evening of that last dreadful day, as Alice, perking up by the minute, flew through the air towards New York at Portia's side, the Playleader crept home, shattered beyond measure. He slept fitfully for a little while, woke up about eleven-thirty, and began to prowl restlessly from room to room of the small apartment, checking in every mirror that he passed how he looked to be taking it. To his dissatisfaction, he saw that he looked only haggard. He felt like death. The excitement of the past week had kept him buoyed up. Now he was sunk fathoms deep. It amazed him that he, who had so deliberately cultivated only small emotions, should feel such a sense of . . . it wasn't loss so much as despair over his Alice-less condition.

The flat was a prison. He heard a clock strike midnight. The strokes seemed to go on and on, many times past twelve. He tried to sleep again and couldn't. Tried to read a book. Couldn't. Made some coffee. Didn't care to drink it. Stared tragically out of the window at the full, wispy harvest moon. He could have bayed it.

An idea popped into his mind. As soon as it did, he recognised that it had been simmering deep down in his consciousness for many weeks. Despair and the moon had brought it to the surface. Healthily invigorated at the prospect of action, he quickly cheered up. Humming to himself, he moved around the flat picking up a few necessaries—an eiderdown, two cushions, some apples, and some other easy-to-carry things. He fed the electric meter three tenpence pieces to keep it going. He splashed some water on Alice's deserted plants. Tongue cutely protruding from the corner of his mouth, he carefully wrote a last message: "NO MILK TILL FURTHER NOTICE THANK YOU". And then he quit his married home without a backward glance.

The park in the very early morning was mysterious and cool and full of scents. Without much difficulty he had hoisted himself and the case he had brought over the fence which separated the park from the road. He travelled by the clear moonlight along the path he took each morning, brushing occasionally into cobwebs but alarming himself only when by accident he kicked over an empty coke can on the gravel.

He climbed through the largest tear in the Playground fence,

and piled his effects beside the door of the hut while he dipped
into his pockets for the keys. For a moment, horribly, he feared
they had fallen out. But then his frantic fist closed on them hidden
in a tuck of his trouser pocket. He opened the door, flicked on the
light, and savoured the smell of earth and rubber that rose from
the equipment stored at the back of the room. Then he turned
and peered out at the playground, superficially strange under the
moon, but down deep more familiar now to him and more dear
than any place else.

He made up his bed by the hut's open door where he could see
when he lay on his back the high branches of the tarzan rope tree.
He did not sleep, but felt at rest. Thoughts of Alice crowded his
mind. They were sombre but sweet, inviting him to gorge himself
on their poignancy. But he did not accept them. He thought them
weak and he had decided to be strong.

He strove to put his mind along a new channel. He let his fancy
roam. Lying in the open night, in the sight of trees and stars and
a great harvest moon, he thought himself, thought himself . . . a
boy scout, in fact. But he quickly kicked that errant notion out and
tried again. A soldier. Much more like it. One of the older sort,
of course; not like now scrabbling in the ruins of Aden or Belfast,
but, perhaps, resting after a mighty night march to the field of war.
Tomorrow the slow mist would disperse, revealing on the opposite
hill the foe, dripping banners and bayonets. The tocsin would
sound. . . . He shivered nervously. Perhaps a safer thought. He was
resting *after* the battle. Indeed, he felt a warm, satisfying glow along
his arm where a sword had grazed him as he led his men cutting
and hacking through the despairing ranks of the enemy.

Alice.

He thought hurriedly of what exact war he was in, whose soldier he was. He sniffed back through history discarding this and
that conflict—too squalid, too tame, ugly uniforms. Cromwell's
war, he decided, fit the bill well. It would explain this English night
certainly, and the outfits, leather jerkins and high boots, had great
appeal. Marston Moor. Naseby. His head throbbed with the tramp
of the New Model Army. He strained to catch the high challenge
of the bugle.

But did they use bugles? He wasn't sure. And anyway the whole war was going a bit cold on him. He didn't really want to be a Roundhead after all. Nor a Cavalier. Crown, Church, Parliament, the whole thing had been a drag; thinking of the rank and bloated present-day equivalents, he'd be damned if he'd risk his life for their seventeenth-century ancestors.

But again memories of Alice threatened to brim over and into his tired mind. Fitfully he scrabbled through the centuries for another war, a better one. He wanted something decently modern and comprehensible, yet one with a touch of old world glamour too, a spice of colour among all the misery. 1914-18 was right out, no hesitation. The Boer War? Faintly ridiculous, as were all those dusty late Victorian fights in Africa. And such base motives behind every one! He went further back. The Crimea. He shuddered under his eiderdown to think of it. How typically sleazy were the wars his poor country got itself into!

So he travelled abroad, since travelling was in the air that night. And at last found himself drifting down in his space-and-time machine upon a broad green valley, piled with forests and clear streams and sunlight, which had wide spaces where birds sang and squirrels and foxes darted about, and other spaces—in the same great valley—where men ran out from behind the forest trees and fired at one another and where rows of cannon thundered and smoked, their shells clawing the ground in front of a long line of men who advanced slowly, gallantly towards the challenging guns.

With a sigh, the Playleader settled contentedly in the midst of the Civil War in America. He had not much to go on—memories of O-level history, an Audie Murphy picture he had seen long ago, *Gone With the Wind* which he had read at nine ("What's rape, Mummy?"). Still, he did his best, and won his wound (from which he was presently recovering) quite convincingly. He did not hog to himself any amazingly gallant action, but took his hurt as one of the common soldiery. The battle took place in Virginia, which sounded a pretty place to die. His colonel rode along the line of waiting infantry.

"Right, boys," called the grand old warrior. "General says to shift those damn rebels off the hill." (The choice of sides had been a momentary problem. But he had his integrity, for Christ's sake, and he was firmly now in blue, his best colour anyway incidentally.) "Bugler sound the charge!"

The notes squealed out upon the beautiful soft air. Drums sounded, the flags were unfurled. The Playleader trotted doggedly forward with his fellows, neither too far in front, nor lagging behind. The enemy was three hundred yards distant across a field bright with young wheat. The rebel artillery played upon the advancing troops. Showers of dirt splattered the Playleader; he quickened and lengthened his stride, clutching his rifle tight. He felt no fear. None. Rifle bullets whined by him. Men fell to the right and left. In bed, in the hut, the Playleader's hand crept protectively over his genitals. But in fact the wound, when it came, arrived deep and comfortable in his stomach. He dropped to his knees upon the rich earth. His lieutenant, coming up from behind, paused to rest a hand upon the Playleader's bowed shoulder.

"Poor brave fellow," cried the officer, young and compassionate. Then he was off like a good soldier to add his weight to the coming clash of arms.

The Playleader gazed up at the blue sky, tenderly holding his abdomen, enjoying the feel of warm blood leaking over his hands. The crash of battle sounded all around him. He could see many dead men from where he lay. Fortunately, none of them had suffered any nasty mutilations; all had died cleanly.

Two stretcher bearers came up to take him away. "Did we win?" he asked them anxiously. His first thought.

"Hard to tell," the man at his head told him. "Many dead on both sides. Great confusion, loss, tragedy. Anyway," he added warmly, tucking the Playleader up nice and comfy on the stretcher. "You done your part, son. By God, you did!"

Now he lay in a field hospital awaiting transport to a proper nursing home in Washington. He was very happy although indeed his tummy was rather sore. For he could see along the labyrinth through which he now dreamed that at the very end of his travail, in the part of the nurse seconded from Mrs Nightingale's pioneer British unit to care for America's war heroes, looking at first just a bit like Virginia McKenna but, as he worked his way towards her, more and more like herself, standing there with forceps in her hand and a smile upon her lovely face, was his own dear Alice.

It was not implausible. She had flown in that direction that very night. He wondered if he could work in a last clinch with her before the curtains closed and the lights went up and the audience filed out of the cinema into the dim, rainy English streets beyond.

Part Three

THE PLAYLEADER'S DAYS fell quickly into a new routine. Most nights he slept at the Playground hut; occasionally he went home to have a bath, pick up more clothes, and check the post. It was easy enough dossing at the hut. He ate at the café nearby, refreshed himself at the park's fountain, and relieved himself in its Gents'. In the evenings he usually read among the stack of comics the kids had left behind or, if a portable set was among Denis's dad's treasure trove in the back of the hut, yawned at the TV shows. Once or twice he went out to the pub, returning a little tiddly late at night, tripping over himself as he blundered along the path to the Playground. No-one bothered him in his retreat.

He was afflicted by a settled melancholy which, though not particularly acute at any one moment, seemed to go on and on and to drain him very deep. Never much inclined to hustle around at his work, now he rarely stirred from his chair outside the hut. His mood seemed to transfer itself to the Playground. In these early autumn days it wore a very different aspect from the noise and colour of its midsummer peak. It was quiet now, few people ran or shouted, many of the ropes—which the Playleader still conscientiously put up every morning—hung unused for long periods. Only the tarzan rope was always in action. A lot of kids simply stayed away, and their absence—with that of the children who had been injured during the quelling of the riot—left the Playground looking empty, lonely, at one with much else in the park that had lived riotously through the summer and now with quiet resignation awaited the coming of the dying season.

Some people though carried on more or less unchanged. Denis and Harmon and their friends had been at an early-season Chelsea away-match at the time of the riot and so had escaped quite unscathed. On the whole, in fact, they felt that the Playground had if anything improved since then, for there were now so many fewer noisy little kids getting in the way. The Playleader got on their nerves a bit, moping around the place as he did. But they found his new habit of living in the hut a definite plus. Often, after the smaller children had gone home, they spent the evening hours lounging round the open hut, watching TV with him and drinking beer. They tried to devise ways of cheering him up and he listened, not entirely without interest in the result, to long discussions about which local woman they could set up for him. Nothing came of it. And once Denis, with a wink and a nudge, shook some little yellow pills in the Playleader's palm, promising him they'd do the trick. He swallowed them, but nothing came of that either. He suspected that the lad had been fobbed off with aspirin.

Still, these evidences of their friendly feelings towards him warmed him. They were the best things about these bad days. Partly because they were unexpected. He had never got along particularly well with most of the older kids, people like Danny and Collins and Facey and others whose names, after a whole summer, he still didn't know. They, he was sure, regarded him as a bit soft, unentitled to his vague position of authority. And ever since the season's disastrous beginning, he had seen them mostly as random muscle behind their leaders' threats. He had not been able easily to react to them as individuals. They were a pack to him, and not a bright one either.

After a few evenings in their company in the hut he was not at all sure what he thought of them. Almost all their conversation, in his hearing at least, was about professional football, most of them being Chelsea fans, with one or two eccentrics following Crystal Palace. The Playleader would have comfortably dismissed them on this basis as incurably limited, except that there was something curiously ritualistic about ninety per cent of their chat so that it seemed more and more to him an elaborate camouflage for whatever more special, more unorthodox thoughts and fancies they might be concealing down there.

For instance, Collins, lounging on a pile of old tyres watching a TV cartoon out of the corner of his eye, might call across to Glen Thompson sitting over by the door, sniffing at a bottle of carpet cleaner fluid (all the rage that summer)—"Wha' 'bout fuckin Osgood then Thompson eh?"

And Glen would call back after a while, "Yeah . . . fuckin Osgood!"

After three or four minutes Collins would say, "Fuckin marvellous eh?"

And Collins, if the carpet cleaner hadn't yet wiped him out, would enthuse back a little later, "Yeah . . . that fuckin Osgood! Fuck!"

And, as the Playleader knew, any of them could ramble on like that about Osgood or some other big-time footballer for an hour's length and more, never shifting out of a basic vocabulary of about a dozen words.

More exciting for the Playleader was their other big topic of conversation (although really it was only a subsidiary to the main one): fighting with the fans of other teams. At this time the glory days of bovver seemed to lie just in the past; it was their slightly older brothers who had fought pitched battles across the centres of Manchester and Liverpool for the honour of Chelsea. Still, they all liked to turn out in force for a match against another London team, whether bawling their defiance from the Chelsea Shed or travelling riotously along the tube line to West Ham and Tottenham and the Arsenal. From these they brought back amazing tales of murderous scuffles in the stands and in the back-streets outside the grounds; stories too of the partiality of the local cops in awarding arrests between the opposing factions; and sometimes they brought back ragged scarves gaudy with the enemy team's colours and occasionally with blood.

"'Ere, wha'd 'e say when ya took 'is scarf?"

"Said 'is fuckin mum 'ad knit it for 'im. Said she'd fuckin do me if I dint fuckin give it back. I fuckin 'it 'im for it. Fuckin Arsenal wanker."

Two or three of the kids who hung around the hut on these pleasant early autumn days weren't into these exciting diversions, in fact weren't into anything very much at all. They spent their time drowsing in the sunshine, their heads nodding, smiling little secret smiles to themselves, and saying to one another in very

slow, very sleepy, slightly surprised voices things like, "He-e-y man
. . . this is *nice* . . . Right?"

They were quite the quietest inhabitants of the Playground. But
somehow they were more obtrusive than any of the others.

With most of the older kids who came to share his evenings
the Playleader got by with a sort of humpily silent approach, swig-
ging a lot of beer, encouraging burps and farts to rise up out of
him, and saying "Shit!" and "Christ!" and so on in a very tough and
pissed-off voice when something particularly terrible occurred on
TV. It seemed to work, one more camouflage among the rest.

With both Denis and Harmon things were more pleasant and
more complicated. Both had a mysterious ability to switch incredibly quickly from the usual kid-stuff droning on about football to
a perceptive and watchful maturity. Denis was the more unset-
tling in this way. Much of the time he was the same cheery young
tough he had been all the time at the beginning of the summer.
But behind this disarming front the Playleader often discerned
a delicate intuitive intelligence at work, surveying him as thoroughly as it did Denis's friends and rivals. Fortunately he seemed
wholly well-disposed towards the Playleader. He had extracted the
reason for the Playleader's present low spirits and spent much time
comforting him with true-life stories of others in his acquaintance
who had got rid of their women and had been all the better for
it. Among them was his father. "Since he sent the old girl back to
Ireland," he reported, "it's bin smiles all the way."

Interestingly, Denis was not an uncritical admirer of his father.
In fact, he took a fairly dim view of the latter's prospects. "He's
greedy all right," he conceded, swallowing his beer, "but he don'
have the *weight*. You should see the blokes he's got workin for
him. One of em, f'rinstance, is that little poof Straker what comes
down here. And you're another, I meantersay!" Denis shook his
head. "The kind of things he's gettin into now, he's gonna get hurt
wiv that lot. I aint stayin around for that."

Harmon seemed to have changed a lot over the summer too,
most obviously in appearance. The old jeans and sleeveless sweaters had been discarded. He turned up now most usually in expen-

sive-looking and shapely dark suits. By contrast his shirts were always in vivid primary colours, often with ruffled fronts, usually with a tie of matching colour. Black socks, black shoes and shades completed the ensemble. He was drinking Scotch mostly now instead of wine and talked often of "When I get my *car* man. . . ."

One unexpected thing about Harmon which the Playleader discovered during this time was that he was a big black power advocate. He, and consequently most of his gang, spent a lot of time over at a black co-operative—housing complex, supermarket, Muslim meeting house—which had been set up in the middle of the dilapidated ghetto beyond one edge of the park from which all of them came. It developed that they saw their home district, with the co-operative in the role of a final redoubt, as a kind of fortress against an attack which they confidently expected at any moment from their white neighbours, spearheaded by the police. "And man, we are *ready* for them," Harmon told the doubting Playleader one night. "*Believe* it! We are *prepared*."

Harmon had a theory—well, he reported it as fact—that there were many more black people in the country than the government dared admit. "Ten million, man, at the *least!*" And though they were in the minority, Harmon had no doubts about the results of the coming struggle for power: "Cause we got *pride*, man and we got *physique* and we got . . . *guns*, man, and we are *ready!*"

This kind of talk usually raised ironic cheers and laughter from the white kids present, in which, after a while, Harmon would usually join, his teeth gleaming cheerily, his eyes hidden behind the shades.

Between Denis and Harmon still existed, the Playleader could tell, some kind of tension, some reticence in their dealings with one another. He asked a couple of questions to try to find out what the matter was, but both of them stonewalled him. So finally he just put it down to a basic incompatibility between the young bulls of different herds.

2

JONATHAN AND TENBY came down to see him one afternoon. Tenby was suitably humble about the events of the day when he was in charge of the Playground. "Those sodding coppers just took off like wild beasts," he tried to explain. "Monstrous abuse of power!"

He was genuinely regretful. The incident had immediately brought down on the Department a considerable amount of extremely unwelcome and unfavourable publicity—press, TV, the works. It had very nearly even precipitated the asking of a question in the House. Tenby had done his best to protect himself, putting the blame in press release on an "inexcusable error of judgement" on the part of the "regular attendant". He had thoughtfully provided too the Playleader's name and address which, printed in full in several papers, had brought a torrent of violent, abusive mail to the Playleader's flat. Even so, some of the shit had stuck to Tenby and in the Department his stock had definitely sunk.

He hoped earnestly that the publication of the book he and Jonathan had put together might recover his fortunes. For a while they had feared that Alice's sudden departure ("Appalling behaviour!" Tenby told the Playleader, clutching his arm in sympathy. "Unnatural!") might mess things up for them at the publishing house. But they had badgered another editor to adopt the book and it would be coming out on schedule after all. They were very hopeful of success. Everything possible was being done. Tenby had already written several reviews for the papers and they were having some luck in persuading the right people to put their names to them.

There was one little item that Tenby wanted to clear up that affected both the book and the Department. It didn't take long. He popped the question with nervous jocularity. The Playleader quickly assured him that, yes, he still did intend to take up the lectureship. And so Tenby, after a cheery farewell, went jauntily upon his way.

The Playleader took Jonathan for a ramble round the hushed Playground.

"I *am* sorry about Alice," Jonathan told him. The Playleader said he didn't really mind.

"Of course you do," Jonathan said sympathetically. Then sensibly refrained from further condolences. They turned at the far fence and made their way back towards the hut.

"I'm sorry in a way you're taking up that job from Tenby," Jonathan said abruptly.

"Why?"

"Oh well . . . because it makes you like everyone else in a way."

The Playleader looked curiously at his companion's handsome face.

"I mean," explained Jonathan, "we're all in that sort of game. At a lowly sort of level . . . writing in shitty magazines or working on lousy TV shows or lecturing somewhere foul or whatever. . . . I used to like to think of you down here, all alone with these kids, swinging in the trees. It just made a nice change to know you. I remember Alice used to tell me about it. She made it sound really fun."

"Bullshit!" the Playleader said crossly. "She liked it so much she never came down here even. I took this crummy lecturing job because of her. She didn't like me down here one bit. She despised it."

"Oh, maybe," Jonathan was taken aback by the Playleader's anger. "I just thought differently . . ." They were silent for a while. Then Jonathan said, "Still. Now she's gone you don't have to leave here."

"It closes in a couple of weeks."

"Well . . . you don't have to go to that university anyway. There'll be next summer. You can come back then. And the summer after that."

They were standing by the gate. The Playleader was a little annoyed at being forced out in the open. "No," he said. "I've thought about it. I have to make my *way* in life. This is young man's stuff. Next year—" He screwed up his face in anguish. "I'll be *twenty-eight!*"

They shook hands sadly. The Playleader held his grip. "Tell

me," he said. "I won't mind. Did you or didn't you? With Alice?"

"Well," said Jonathan awkwardly, disengaging his hand. "Just one little one. But before I met you. Promise."

Another visitor to the Playground in its closing days was Frank. He came twice in fact, both times looking for the elusive Straker.

"I really haven't seen him," the Playleader told him on the second time. "Why *should* he be here?"

"You're still storing things for Riley?" Frank asked as he peered into one after the other of the children's now mostly untenanted shanties.

"I suppose so," the Playleader agreed. The TV sets and record players were still moving into and out of the hut in a steady stream. "But Straker isn't dealing with them. There's a lot of different blokes now. Mostly Irish. I had a Cypriot last evening."

"Straker's still working for Riley," Frank told him shortly. "He'll be down here sooner or later." He came to the end of his search and threw up his hands in rage and despair. "Fuckit!" he cried at the pale sun. "I'm through with chasin after 'im. Let 'im fry. I don't care!"

The Playleader prevailed on the big man to accept some of Harmon's Scotch. Frank agreed. They sipped their drinks leaning on opposite posts of the hut's door. Frank was very blue. Not only Straker, it seemed, had strayed from the straight and narrow.

"None of em come down to Rube's hardly anymore," he complained. "Just Isobel and me sittin there lookin stoopid. It's breakin her heart, never mind me." He kicked at a nearby rock, revealed his most painful wound. "We aint gonna be able to take up our share of seats this year on the Eddie Cochran excursion. Gordon aint comin. I can't get hold of Straker." He looked moodily across at the Playleader. "What about you?" he grunted. "You interested? Two weeks from Tuesday. Coach trip to the hospital where Eddie passed on. Tea at the Ace Café. And a special showing of *The Girl Can't Help It* at the Camberwell ABC. Quid the lot."

The Playleader thought it over. Then shook his head. "I wish I could," he said regretfully. "But I have to dine at high table in my College that evening." Frank spat in the dust.

Later he said, "I'm so fuckin *tired.*" In the low streaming September sun, sitting propped up against a door-post, the big man slept, his mouth disconsolately drooping open. The Playleader removed Frank's empty glass from his hand and looked down compassionately at his thinning pompadour. When Facey and Thompson came rollicking into the Playground twenty minutes later, the Playleader put his forefinger warningly to his lips. And silently the two boys negotiated Frank's sprawling form in the door of the hut, picking their way with delicate exactitude between the long legs encased in their brilliant blue drainpipe trousers.

Finally, Straker did appear in the Playground, very early one morning when the Playleader was still asleep. Straker shook him by the shoulder. "I heard you was kippin down here," he said. "I couldn't believe it. But here you are!"

The Playleader sat up blinking. Straker put into his hands a mug of tea he had brought from the café. "Where've you been?" the Playleader asked, sipping the drink. "What are you here for?"

"I been away," Straker told him, settling himself on the floor. He peered warily out at the Playground. "I been up in Liverpool, as a matter of fact. Weird place! Here"—he plunged his hand into his pocket—"I got something for you. A souvenir." He handed over a photograph. It showed two women fondling each other's genitals, one of them was sipping at the other's left tit. "There," said Straker complacently, "I remembered your little kinks see?"

The Playleader studied the little man with interest. His appearance had undergone a sea-change. His hair was now razor-cut very close to his head, very styled in the Italian manner. And his Ted clobber had been exchanged for a brand-new slightly flashy version of a conventional business suit. Underneath he wore a white shirt, with a button-down collar and sort of club tie.

Straker preened himself under the Playleader's inspection. "Like it?" he asked. He tapped the upper pocket of his jacket. "I got the shades in there too if I need em."

"Frank's looking for you," the Playleader told him. Straker wrinkled up his nose.

"Aaah! Him!" he snorted.

"He's worried about you. He thinks you're in some kind of trouble."

"Fuckin nursemaid! Who needs him?"

The Playleader was astonished. "I thought you were good friends," he cried.

Straker shrugged. "I *respect* Frank. I *like* Frank," he said, clearly trying to be fair. "But Christ! I'm through wiv all that hangin around in back-street cafés! I've bin findin out what I've bin missin over these past few weeks. I've bin findin out about *night-clubs*. I've bin findin out about *casinos*. He's held me back all these years, Frank. You wouldn't believe how much he's held me back."

The Playleader shook his head. "How much has he?"

"Guess how much I made last month wiv Riley?" Straker urged.

"Oh . . . *money*," said the Playleader, deprecatingly.

"Yeah, *money*! Fuckin good money an all. Go on . . . guess how much."

"Dunno."

"About three fifty, that's all. How about that? That's how much Frank has held me back. About three fifty last month, more like four this. That's how much."

The Playleader finished his tea. He gazed once more at the little man opposite him. "It's sad though," he said.

"What's sad?" asked Straker. "Not for me it aint."

"Oh I remember you in that Ted get-up and all your rock'n'roll chat. It was just nice. You existing like that."

"All very well," said Straker. "Very nice for the spectators. But I got to make my way in life you know." The phrase was familiar.

"Tough on Frank though," said the Playleader. "Nobody's coming out for the Eddie Cochran trip."

Straker flushed guiltily. "Well," he said quickly, "business an all." He lit a cigarette moodily. "Look, I got *nothin* against Eddie Cochran," he said urgently. "Frank should know that. But . . . but"—he finished up in a rush—"there's a lot to be said for Tom Jones and Lulu too."

Later, when Straker was about to go, the Playleader said, "Well, I'll tell Frank if I see him you were here and you're all right."

"Yeah," Straker said. "Tell him I said hello." He scratched his well-shod shoe in the Playground dust. "Tell him I'll be down at Rube's one of these fine days."

At the gate the Playleader said, "Well, I guess I won't be seeing you again."

Straker looked up at him in surprise. "Course you will," he said. Then checked himself. "Jesus! I didn't tell you. That's what I came to say. I'll be in tonight sometime."

"What for?"

"Got a parcel to bring in. Usual stuff."

"Well . . . when are you coming?"

"Late in the night. Or early morning. You'll be in?"

"Yeah. The door'll be open anyway. You don't have to wake me if I'm asleep."

Straker leaned over the wire fence and gave the Playleader's cheek a merry squeeze. "You sly fing," he said, playfully. "I'll wake you wiv a little kiss if you're not careful!"

3

IN THE AFTERNOON of the same day the Playleader was ambling back from the café to the park, mind blank and stomach pretty full. Over the summer he had become a regular at the café and so now he always got the overheaped platefuls befitting his favoured status.

As he prepared to cross the road opposite the park gates, the black man laid a hand gently upon his arm. "Into the car," he said, firmly but not unpleasantly.

The Playleader saw parked just to his left a white Jaguar. The rear door next to the pavement was open. "Oh God!" he cringed. And to the man who held him. "I got no money, please . . . !"

"Just get *in*," the man said and propelled him gently into the car. One man was at the driver's seat, another in the rear. The man who had picked him up got into the back seat too and closed the door. The Playleader sat uncomfortably in the middle. There was surprisingly little room in the Jag.

They drove off.

"Oh shit!" mumbled the Playleader, looking imploringly at the impassive black faces on either side of him.

Nothing was said for about five minutes as the car penetrated deep into the narrow little streets of the black ghetto. Through the window the Playleader could see the gathering tide of storefront churches, West Indian groceries, and people lounging and playing cards on the steps outside the tenements. The driver turned a knob on the dashboard and, improbably, the strains of Mantovani filled the car. Then the man on the Playleader's right, who had been in the car when he got in, leaned towards him.

"Now don't you *worry*," the man said in a deep, attractive, lilting voice. His breath, so close, smelled sickeningly of violets. "Nobody wants ta hurt ya, and we'll put you back where you belong in just a little while."

The Playleader peeked over at the man on his other side who smiled at him encouragingly. The man on his right spoke again. "Now. You work down in that playground down there in the park, don't you? In fact," his voice rose slightly in his incredulity, "I *heah* you even *sleep* there."

The Playleader nodded. It was so.

"And I heah too you keep things in there for a guy called Riley. Is that *right*? Huh?"

The Playleader blew out his lips in exasperation. "For Christ's sake!" he groaned. "It's just a bunch of domestic appliances! And a little parcel once in a while. Junk!"

"That's right," the man said easily. "Junk. Now . . . you also know a guy called Straker?"

The Playleader was silent. The man on his right gripped his arm.

"Hey," he said, "don't even *tink* of holdin anythin back."

"Oh all right, I know him," the Playleader admitted. The man let him go. The Playleader rubbed his arm. "But he's perfectly harmless," he told them.

"He's a *freak*!" said the man on his left contemptuously. The Playleader turned to argue with him; the man on his right pulled him back.

"I aint finished," he said gently. He caressed the Playleader's sore arm. "I want you to tell me," he said, "just when you plan to see this Straker guy again."

Once more the Playleader was silent. The man on his right sighed deeply. The stench of violets was overwhelming. The driver, looking in the rear-view mirror, caught the Playleader's eye. "Hey, don't fuck around with us," he advised. "You tell the man what he wants to know."

"What are you going to do to him?" the Playleader quavered. The man on the right smacked him hard in the mouth. "He's coming tonight to the hut," the Playleader breathed, tears in his eyes. "Or early in the morning."

"Tha's better," said the man who had hit him, his arm comfortably around the Playleader's shoulders. "OK," he said to the driver. "Back we go!" He was in high spirits. The Playleader dabbed at his mouth with a grubby handkerchief.

They drove for a while in silence. Then the man on his right said, "I believe you know my boy Harmon? I believe he spends time down at your place."

The Playleader peered up at the man. "You're Harmon's *father*?" he asked faintly.

"I'm his *uncle*," said the man. "He aint got a father. But I look out for him. How's he doin?"

"Oh . . . fine," said the Playleader, speaking with some difficulty.

"Tha's good," said Harmon's uncle. "He's a good boy."

"A natural leader," said the Playleader warming to the task.

"Is that right?" The man on his right nodded contentedly. "He comes from good blood that boy. I'd be surprised if he turned out different."

They drew up beside the park. "OK," said Harmon's uncle, opening his door. The Playleader clambered over his legs to get out and away. But the man held onto his arm so that he had to stand on the curb half in and half out of the car.

"I jus' wanted to say," Harmon's uncle told him seriously, sounding even a little shy, "thank you from myself and from the whole community for the good work you're doin down heah with our kids."

"It's OK," faltered the Playleader, his tears falling like rain. "Just my job."

"Right," Harmon's uncle nodded, "nice meeting you." And he let go of the Playleader, who jumped back onto the pavement and then scuttled terrified into the park.

4

He thought of going down to Rube's to tell Frank. He thought of looking for Straker to warn him. Or finding Denis to pass the word on to his father. In the end he did nothing. As the afternoon wore on and the alarming events at lunch-time receded from his immediate consciousness he couldn't believe that anything *really* serious and dangerous was in the offing. It was the collection of Riley's stuff in the back of the hut which mostly helped to allay his fears. Today's lot was a particularly scrappy one: two vacuum cleaners, three very plastic-looking radio sets and—a new low—a dusty and dented washing machine. Not a stereo or a TV set among them.

Looking at these, he began to suspect that an elaborate joke was being played upon someone. Him, perhaps? The idea that serious trouble could arise over such a collection made him laugh out loud—an action which made his hurt mouth smart terribly. He frowned and resolved to tell Harmon next time he saw him that, joke or no joke, his uncle had altogether stepped over the mark.

None of the kids looked in to see him that evening. He read a comic book called *Gargantua the Planet Killer* which Collins had lent him for a while. Then for some hours he devoted himself to filling in a few of the scores of densely printed forms which had been sent on by his future university employers. By twelve o'clock Straker had still not arrived. But the Playleader felt sleepy, and, after a trip to the drinking fountain to brush his teeth, he crawled inside his sheets and pulled the eiderdown over his head.

Lying in the dark, his fears revived. Something was up, he knew it, some trouble was coming to a head. However absurd the source of the quarrel, those men in the car had meant business. He should have found some way to warn Straker. He knew it now. Something bad was going to happen. A beating most probably. Even now, he thought, he could get up, run out into the park, make a commotion, possibly scare off both the intending assailants and their intended victim. But he didn't. Cursing his cowardice, he crouched deeper into the warm bed-sheets. For punishment, he flogged his imagination on to picture even worse fates for Straker. Mere beatings-up were soon left far behind. Across the Playleader's tired and excited mind swept frantic visions of knotted ropes, and knives, and—most clearly, most persistently—guns. Revolvers, shotguns, machine guns. All pointing at his friend's frail little body. He fell asleep convinced beyond a doubt that he would awake to the thrilling crash of gunfire in the night.

In fact, he woke to the smell of violets in the early morning. Harmon's uncle stood over him, peering down upon him, filling the doorway with his big frame so that to the Playleader's dazed waking vision he seemed like a god occupying the whole sky. Focusing hastily upon this apparition, he was relieved to see him smiling, looking in fact hugely exuberant.

"Hel-*lo!*" the man cried. "We were passin by. So we thought to visit." He plumped himself down on a chair revealing, standing behind him, his nephew, who acknowledged the Playleader with a shy grin. "We aint bin to bed all night," Harmon's uncle said. "We bin *busy*. Right, boy?"

"Tha's right," Harmon nodded.

The uncle looked down contemplatively at the Playleader, who was hurriedly sorting his upper half into a sweater. "You missed a *lot* of action last night," he said.

The Playleader lit a cigarette with a trembling hand. "What happened?" he asked painfully.

"Why, your friend had some bad luck near heah."

The Playleader's heart went cold. He looked across imploringly to Harmon.

"That bent bloke Straker got done by the law," Harmon explained.

"Tha's right," his uncle gleamed. "Somebody tipped them off.

They picked him up jus' out in the road there outside the park. Easy as pie."

"What for?" the Playleader asked. "Why should they?"

"On account of the little parcel he was carrying, I should say. Wouldn't you?"

"Why? What was in it?"

The uncle and the nephew looked at each other. The nephew smiled. The uncle said in a tone of great contempt, "Why, smack, man, what else? *You* know. The white lady."

"Oh . . . shit!" cried the Playleader, collapsing back upon his pillow.

The uncle looked down on him and shook his head. "I can't hardly *believe* you're such an *ass*-hole."

"I told you he dint know *nothin*," Harmon said.

"You mean all those little parcels that have been going in and out of here all summer contained . . ." The Playleader couldn't finish.

"I guess so," nodded Harmon's uncle soberly. "I guess they did."

"But what were all those TV sets and radios and everything about?"

The uncle laughed derisively. "That fuckin Riley! He's got a half-dozen little stashes like this one heah and he switches all that crap aroun' from one to the other. But only *one* had the goods in it. *Yours.* It was s'posed to fool us. . . . Did for a while too. The creep!"

"It fooled me *all* the time," the Playleader said sadly.

"Yeah, so I see," the uncle said curtly. He popped a violet tablet in his mouth. The Playleader lit another fag, shaking his head.

"*You* turned Straker in?" he asked.

"Tha's right."

"Why? Why would you do that?"

"Cause nobody deals smack aroun' heah except *us*."

Harmon spoke up. "Fuckin Riley was trying to cut in."

"It's not that we're greedy," the uncle explained, "but if we don' keep our territory in order, then our sources don' come through for us. You know Eye-talians. Excitable. But they like order in business. We provide it. Now *you* see we couldn't be allowin amateurs like this Riley and Straker messin aroun' with stuff they don' know nothin' about. Not aroun' heah. *You* unnerstan' that."

The Playleader asked anxiously, "Do you think he'll get a long sentence?"

The uncle, beaming, spread his arms out to their furthest breadth. "For heroin? Years!" he cried, making the word spread over many seconds. "*De*-cades!"

The Playleader looked down moodily at his cigarette. "It seems so unfair," he mourned. "Poor little cunt. He was just trying to help himself up. Did you have to do it to him?"

"Bullshit!" exploded the uncle, leaping up from his chair, shaking his finger wrathfully at the Playleader. "Listen man," he cried, "I'm the fuckin voice of moderation aroun' heah. I want you to know that. Harmon'll tell you." The boy nodded quickly. "Harmon'll tell you they's a lot of people wanted this Straker knocked off. *Killed*. Tha's right. An this Riley too. Yeah. But I said *no*. I said no, we aint doin that. And not"—he waggled his finger again—"not because I give a shit for those creeps but because"—he sank back into his chair, smiling again—"because what the fuck? What's the point? Riley'll get the idea. He'd better! This way there's no mess to clear up. Everything's cool." He looked down at the Playleader and said seriously, "You oughta be *thankin* me man."

But the Playleader had another worry on his mind. "If the cops have him," he said, "they'll find out about this hut. I'll be—Jesus! I'll be an *accessory*!"

The uncle shook his head. "He won't say nothin to the cops," he promised. "He wouldn't dare. He knows if he says a thing about where he was takin the stuff, where he got it from—anythin at all that might get back to Riley and whoever's in back of their whole thing, well. . . ." The uncle drew a finger across his broad black neck. "An he wouldn't have to wait for it till he got back outside neither."

The Playleader nodded glumly, "Well that's a relief anyway," he said.

The uncle leaned a little closer. "On the other han'," he said carefully, "There's nothin at all to stop me givin the cops a tip on my own account. But anonymous of course. About you and this hut heah and what you bin keepin in it *all* summer . . ."

"But why would you *do* such a thing?" trembled the Playleader.

The uncle grinned at him. "Why, I *wouldn't*," he cried. "I *wouldn't* . . . Long as you don't ever say *nothin* about *anythin*. You understan'? You say a word. One word. Tha's all. An we . . ."

The Playleader shook his head furiously. "I won't say *anything*," he promised fervently. "I won't even *think* anything."

"Tha's right," the uncle said warmly, stooping to pat the Playleader's shoulder. "You a good boy."

Harmon shuffled impatiently by the door. "Hey, I wanta get along now," he said.

"OK," the uncle stood up. "I'm comin with you."

Uncle and nephew bade the Playleader friendly goodbyes. But he hardly noticed, he was too occupied with mourning Straker's wretched fate. "Where d'you think they'll put him?" he sighed.

The uncle considered. "Parkhurst maybe," he said gently. "You can make a day of it."

The uncle paused at the door. "You get along," he told Harmon, "I'll catch you up." For a while he stood and watched the Playleader's grief sympathetically. But then, evidently, an errant thought came to his mind. His expression changed. He began to grin delightedly.

"Shit, man!" he cried to the Playleader's bowed head. "Don't you mourn for *him*! You *know* the way those boys in jail carry on. Your little frien' is goin to think he's landed in *paradise* with all them big prison queens! He won' want to come *out*!" And he began to expand his vision of Straker's juicy future as the morning lightened behind him, interpolating his account with laughter so glorious and infectious that the Playleader, genuine though his regret was, could not help after a little while giggling madly along with him.

5

ON THE DAY after the Playground closed for the winter, the Playleader came down to pick up a few things of his own from the hut. It was full autumn and, in some ways, the Playground looked

brighter now with the season's colours in every tree than it had
during the last tired weeks it was open. The Playleader wandered
about, picking up a few broken toys, thinking to himself how little
a space the Playground seemed to occupy, so much smaller now
that he was, practically, out of it.

By the great tree in the centre of the Playground which had
held the tarzan rope he paused and gazed up at the high branches
to which he had had to climb every morning all summer long . . .
Well, every morning but one. Smiling, he remembered how Portia
had swung from the great rope, shrieking, twisting, jerked out of
her habitual cool by its wild traverse.

He thought too, inevitably, of Portia's lover. He had heard twice
from Alice since their departure. First a card from New York, brief
and very bright: "94 degrees here and humid to boot! All is *fantastic*. Portia sends her—well she does! People keep feeling my BUM
in the street!!!" Later he had got an air-letter, also with a New York
postmark. He opened it with bounding hopes. But it was almost
entirely to do with some vast political imbroglio that apparently
was currently staggering the city, involving Mayor Lindsay, Gov-
ernor Rockefeller, three instructors from City College, a gay com-
mune on Grove Street, "those fuckin know-nothin up-state apple
pickers", and lots of other minor actors, none of whom he knew
or cared about. The letter did not come from any Alice he had ever
known. He threw it away.

He got slightly more information about his wife's progress
in the New World by visiting every week a bookseller in Char-
ing Cross Road which carried air-mail editions of foreign under-
ground papers. Portia's journal was on sale there and he read her
column—re-titled "Sexiles' Return"—religiously. It was clear that
she and "A" were still very much together. Tremendous passion
throbbed in every line of Portia's prose. How bitterly the Playleader begrudged her the "sight of A after a night of shameless
blameless lust all tits and downy ass and sweet confusion in the
morning sun"!

Still, one or two items gave him a twinge of malicious pleasure.
Clearly "A" was having a little too much fun these days for her
mentor: "shit flies all morning today my lively london lassie is sud-

denly become a *very heavy* political lady indeed spends all her time
down on grove st with H and K and other charmers O we just talk
she says in that bland beautiful way O yeah? I say till 3 am you just
talk? I mean I know those chicks hon and you aint just *talkin* and
so on and so on and jesus! I have to get my shit together and get
myself and herself back to the coast very fuckin soon. . . ."

But there wasn't really much hope there for him. And what
there was would take so long to mature. And after all . . . well,
perhaps he didn't have the time to spare. He sensed in himself with
interest during these latter days the stirring of a small rebellion.
It was time, he thought, to change out of this celibate mourning
stuff. If she didn't want him . . . OK, thousands did. Well . . . there
might well be one or two who did. He had growing hopes of the
university. Seven out of the sixteen who had so far signed up for
his course were women. If they wanted good marks . . . And there
were bound to be lady dons hanging around. Bound to be . . . Or
other lecturers' wives. . . .

He continued cheerfully on his ramble, thinking these pleasant thoughts until a child's high voice, crying out his name, inter-
rupted them. He looked up and to his delight saw the little girl he
knew as Gloria's friend hobbling towards him, waving a National
Health crutch in greeting. He hastened to meet her. They met,
blushed, looked each other up and down.

"How's your leg?" he asked.

"All right," she said, "getting on."

He took one of her crutches and she leaned her hand on his
arm for support. Like maiden aunt and favourite nephew they
began to walk slowly across the Playground.

"I dint think you'd be here," she said, "I thought it was closed."

"It is," he said, "this is my last time here."

"You coming back next year?"

"No," he said.

"I aint neither," she said, "I'm movin to Loughborough."

"Why?"

"That's where we're goin to live," she explained. "My mum's
marrying this man she got through an agency. He's from Loughborough, you see."

"What's he like?" the Playleader asked. It was an effort to keep his pace down to hers.

"He's all right," she conceded, "he gives me money. I don't mind 'im."

"Will you like living up there?"

"I'll be glad to leave that at any rate," she said, jerking a crutch at the tall towers of the Herbert Morrison Buildings. "I'm frightened every night they're goin to fall down. One did, you know."

They rested by the hut.

"Why aint you comin back?" she asked curiously.

He shrugged. "I got another job."

"Dint you like it here then?"

He thought for a moment, then shook his head. "No. I thought I liked it for a while. But I never really did. . . . And I wasn't much good at it either."

"You were all right," she urged.

"No."

"Everybody had a good time. That's the main thing."

He shook his head again, doubtfully.

After a while she said, "I got to go home for dinner now."

They set off slowly for the gate. When they reached it, and she was propped up on both crutches again, they shook hands solemnly.

"Goodbye," she said politely, "nice to have known you."

"Yeah," he said. "Enjoy Loughborough now."

6

THE VERY LAST person the Playleader saw while he still actually was one was the Park-keeper who, as he prepared to leave the Playground for the last time, came rollicking in from his lunch.

The Playleader let by-gones be by-gones and shook the old man's hand firmly. "Goodbye," he said, "I'm off now. I won't be back."

The Park-keeper clutched him in drunken desperation. "Don't go," he quavered. "The buggers have given you a hell of a time,

but we need young men like you here. Fine young men! Stay,
boy!"

The Playleader shook his head, partly to clear it from the strong
fumes the old boy had breathed over him, partly to say no, he
really couldn't. But the Park-keeper in his drunken animation now
had him in an iron grip. He had to listen.

"Look," the old fool hissed into the Playleader's wilting ear.
"Listen! You come back next year. You'll see! We'll have a nice surprise for you. You see all that *shit* over there, lad? All that *coal*?"
He waved his arm in a broad arc to cover all of the massive negro
slum that sprawled menacingly over the low hills beyond the park.
Was it imagination, or had it grown measurably since the summer
began? "You see," the man who held him blathered on. "Next year.
Nothing left! That's the word. By next summer. Wiped out! That's
a *promise*!"

The old man was shaking in prophetic fury. His hand had
dropped from the Playleader's arm, but the Playleader stayed on,
regarding the Park-keeper with mounting curiosity and alarm.
He remembered young Harmon's fears. Did this old brute know
something? Was some appalling massacre being planned? The old
man's foaming lips quivered. He was about to utter. The Playleader held his breath.

"'Scuse me," the Park-keeper mumbled. He darted into the
flower-bed, and as he stood, huddled, pissing on to the beautiful
late blossoms, the Playleader took his opportunity to escape for
ever.